I0611022

Other Books

By Lori L. Lake

ROMANCES

Eight Dates (2014)
Like Lovers Do (2011)
Different Dress (2003)
Ricochet in Time (2001)

THE GUN SERIES

Gun Shy (2001)
Under The Gun (2002)
Have Gun We'll Travel (2005)
Jump The Gun (2013)
Gunpoint (forthcoming)

THE PUBLIC EYE MYSTERY SERIES

Buyer's Remorse (2011)
A Very Public Eye (2012)

HISTORICAL NOVELS

Snow Moon Rising (2006)

COLLECTIONS

Shimmer and Other Stories (2007)
Stepping Out: Short Stories (2004)

ANTHOLOGIES EDITED

*Time's Rainbow: Writing Ourselves Back
Into American History (2017)

*Lesbians on the Loose: Crime Writers on the Lam (2015)

*Romance for Life (2005)

*The Milk of Human Kindness: Lesbian Authors Write about
Mothers and Daughters (2004)

Praise for the Stories of
Lori L. Lake

"Lori L. Lake has a flawless ear for the witty twists of the English language and a fine grasp of popular culture. She fearlessly situates her characters in a range of places, times, and dilemmas that might daunt a less gifted and confident author. Readers can relax, knowing they will be carried along by a born story teller."
~Ann Bannon, author of the ground-breaking Beebo Brinker Chronicles

"Lake...cared for and nurtured [her characters], making this not so much a collection of stories as an anthology of characters."
~Lambda Book Report

"[A]n insightful collection of short stories… [E]ach story brings forth interesting characters and situations you long to know more about."
~The Independent Gay Writer, Vol II, Issue 4

"There is an interesting mixture of characters and situations in this book of short stories by Lake. Some I liked better than others, but all were thought provoking. Short stories are tough to get right, and Lake has some skill in bringing the story quickly to life through character, and introducing the scene and plot with enough detail to be vivid and yet not too much to weigh down the brevity of the tale. Not all the tales were uplifting, but none were depressing. It is very hard to find lesbian characters in short stories that aren't classified as erotica. I really enjoyed these quietly queer tales."
~Pippa, Amazon reader

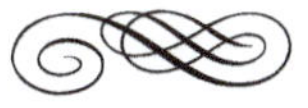

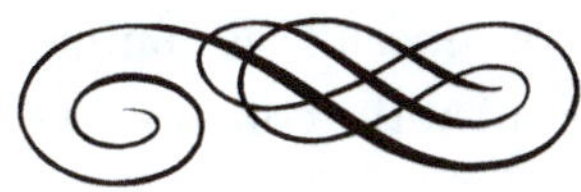

Stepping Out

Short Stories

by

Lori L. Lake

2021

Portland, Oregon
www.LaunchPointPress.com

Dedicated to my late mother, Sylvia Palm, who always wanted me to be a writer and told me I was going to college before I even understood what college was.

Thanks, Mom

Acknowledgments

These stories were a long time in the making, and over the years, many people have helped—not just with the editing and proofing, but also with various kinds of writing guidance and inspiration.

The list includes: Carol Bly, Ruth Boetzel, Mary D. Brooks, Lindsey Bullard, C.A. Casey, Barb Coles, Betty J. Crandall, Ron Donaghe, Nann "Pruferblue" Dunne, Lynne Franklin, Marge Grahn-Bowman, Susan Thurston Hamerski, George Hamm, Ellen Hart, Lois Hart, Reagan Hnetka, MaryAnn Howard, Marilyn Jacaway, Judith Katz, Denise Karamafrooz, Anna and Albert LaCompte, Ian Graham Leask, Rosalie Maggio, Ruth and Walt Manning, Carolyn McBride and Betty Harmon, Joyce McNeil, Kim Miller, Marilyn Orr, Day Petersen, my webmaster Angela Reese, Patty Schramm, "Hydraulic Woman" Kristen Schuldt, Maureen Shaffer, Jean Stewart, Karen "Kas" Surtees, Peg Thompson, Michael Welch, Marie Sheppard Williams, and my judicious buddy Norma.

It's sobering to consider that since the first edition of this collection was published, seven of the people above have died. I still think of them nearly every day and miss them very much.

Special thanks: to the late Donna Pawlowski (another friend who I still miss to this day) who created the cover for the first edition of this collection; to Norcroft: A Writing Retreat for Women where three of these stories were written; to the wonderful folks at The Loft Literary Center in Minneapolis; and to everyone at the old Amazon Feminist Bookstore Co-op in Minneapolis, Minnesota. Long you'll be missed!

In my original 2004 acknowledgments, I thanked my then-partner, Diane. Alas, we did not stay together to celebrate our 75th anniversary as I'd hoped back then, but for nearly three decades she gave me unwavering support, shared my dreams and helped me believe I could actually achieve a writing life. For that, I'll be forever grateful to her.

Lori L. Lake
2004 Version Updated
January 2021

Contents

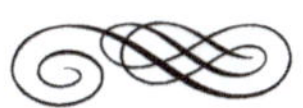

Foreword
By Jean Stewart

Stepping out implies the beginning of a journey, and each of these fourteen stories touches on that theme in its own unique and winding way. Using acute intuitive perception and her evocative ability with words, Lori Lake takes you along a series of intriguing paths. You will meet people you may or may not have met before, and you'll wander into places you will probably remember long after this volume has been passed on to a friend, or kept aside in a nook on that special shelf for the books you'll save forever.

Good stories reach deep inside of you and resonate. There's that sense of knowing something new which, strangely, seems to have been there all along. "Afraid of the Dark" brings us face to face with a topic that many in our politically correct society would rather avoid, as if avoiding this enduring source of despair makes life easier for any of us; this story alone is worth the price of the book. "Propane" is an unflinching gaze into a life many of us do not want to see, or acknowledge, where one partner's power is sustained by the other partner's loss. "The Bright Side" is a rendering of a timely theme: aging parents and a grown-child dealing with the rewards and difficulties of self-definition; this is an exquisitely shaded work. "The Big Eddy" is a walk in a pair of shoes that most of us hope we will never have to wear; but it is one of the most beautifully written and endearing short stories I have ever read.

"Vagabonds" is a rendering of the value of one life and is heartbreak-ingly funny. "Busybody" is a glimpse into the frailty of perceptions, and the value of making connections with unlikely people. "Jumping Over My Head" is a study in choosing to be brave when you are not, a study in daring to think you can do what your head tells you cannot be done; I love this story. "My Lifesaving Journal" is a multi-leveled account of a woman's discovery of her own self-worth; the last few paragraphs of this story are wondrous. "The Jungle Garden," a fond goodbye to a grandmother, is interwoven with the emotional intricacies of family politics; I love this one, too. These and the other five stories here are tales you may find yourself recalling throughout the course of a busy day, or maybe even in the years afterward, for this is that kind of writing.

Beyond the mechanics of good storytelling, a sturdy vulnerability surfaces in every one of these short stories. Lori Lake must possess, simply as part of her inherent nature, a loving heart. It gleams out from these stories, even the sad ones, like a lamp in a lighthouse—maybe far away sometimes, maybe just a passing, slanting flash in the dark—but there to be seen all the same. It makes for a bittersweet journey.

Jean Stewart
Federal Way, Washington
February, 2004

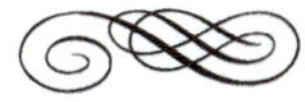

The soul is constantly about to starve: it cannot
live on fun alone. If the soul gets no other food, it
will first tear apart other creatures . . . then itself.

—Selma Lagerlöf (1858-1940)

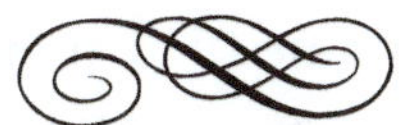

The Bright Side

In the dazzling light pouring from the noon sun, the front of Mel's parents' gray two-story house looked shabby and washed out. The cedar shake siding showed cracks, and as she drew closer to the cement steps, Mel noticed the trim also needed scraping and painting. She shifted her mini-daypack to her left hand and opened the screen door. After a quick tap with the rusting knocker, she turned the doorknob, stepped into the cool front room, and shut the door behind her.

From down the hall she heard the TV. "Mom?" she called out. "Dad?" She glanced around the house, wondering where her parents' scruffy little poodle was.

She set her bag on the rocking chair near the window and stood marveling at how a visit home was like stepping into the past, into a museum of family antiquities and new acquisitions. The living room was an odd mix of new and old. Long gone was the old couch, kept for over fifteen years, that Mel, her twin sister Izzy, and their older brother Nate had bounced on, entertained friends from, and slept upon when they were sick. Ten years ago, the same month Mel and Izzy turned twenty, her parents bought something new. Overstuffed, pale rose in color, and covered in a satiny material, it sat, resplendent, and entirely unused. When it was first delivered, Mel sat on it and found it comfortable, but she'd never touched it again.

The new sofa was quite the contrast to the old shag carpet, meticulously kept up, but ugly cocoa brown just the same. Mel's eyes scanned the room. The same circa 1950 knockoff Goya paintings. The same wingback chairs on either side of a never-used fireplace containing two well-dusted ornamental logs and a clear glass pitcher of fake pink flowers. The ancient German beer steins on the mantel. A lighted corner cabinet contained her mother's collection of Birds of Prey. Eagles, falcons, owls, kestrels—Mel wasn't even sure what all the various figurines were, though her mother, who was a member of various associations like the Raptor Research Foundation and The Peregrine Fund, could name each of them and discuss their habitat, prey, and mating rituals. Mel had always thought her mother should have worked at a zoo.

Following the distant, tinny sound of a laugh track, she moved through the living room, down a narrow hallway, and to the doorway of her parents' bedroom.

"Dad?"

The double bed was made, and a white-haired man lay on top of the bedspread reclining against a stack of pillows, his head tilted slightly to the side. He opened his eyes. "Ahhh . . ." A sharp cough cleared his throat. "Hi, honey. Come on in. I was just watching a little TV." He scooted up, wiped at his mouth with his pale fingertips, and waved toward a white wicker chair on the opposite side of the bed. "Where's your mother?"

"I don't know." Mel shrugged, then sat. "She didn't answer when I came in."

He picked up the remote from on top of the flowered spread and hit the mute. From her seat, Mel saw a TV game show was playing, but she wasn't sure which one it was. Somebody had apparently won a new refrigerator, and the woman was jumping up and down with her over-large bosom coming close to hitting her voluminous chin.

Her father wore olive green khakis, a white button up shirt, and a black sweater. Mel squinted and saw a splotch of something yellow on the chest of the shirt, but before she could ask about it, he said, "So what are you up to today? Off work?"

"No, it's my lunch hour, Dad. You called and asked that I stop by."

"What?" He frowned. "I asked—" He turned back to the TV. "You kids always get what I want confused with what your mother wants. You mean your mother called." He hit the channel select, and Mr. Rogers' face popped onto the screen. "Look there, Mel. Mr. Rogers. Did you hear he died? Why, I was floored. That guy's younger than me!"

Confused, Mel looked down into her lap. What was going on with her father? He *seemed* fine, just like old times, but lately he'd taken to saying or doing odd things, then refusing to admit it later. Before she could ponder it further, she heard a noise, and then a yip-yip-yipping. Pete, newly clipped, came tearing into the room and launched up at the foot of the bed, hitting the end of the mattress and scrabbling wildly with his rear paws. Once safely up, he stopped, startled, and looked at Mel as though she were a ghost. Then with a bark of glee, he came to the edge of the bed nearest to her and turned around in a circle, panting and wagging with excitement.

"Hiya, Petey," she said. She stood and reached over to pet the poodle's head, scratching him behind the ears.

From the doorway she heard her mother's voice. "Well, well, what are you doing here, Imelda?"

"Hi, Mom. I just stopped by for a visit on my lunch hour." Her mother had never called her by anything other than her given name, and Mel hated it. When she was fourteen, the shoe queen, Imelda Marcos of the Philippines, went on trial. Ninth graders are a rude lot, and Mel was teased. She decided that once she grew up, at her first opportunity she'd change her name. Of course, that was back when she thought she might get married one day and easily obtain a new name. By age twenty she knew that wasn't a reality, and she'd never gotten around to filing the paperwork to dump her old-fashioned name.

She stepped away from Pete, and the little dog turned and scurried the few feet to nestle under Nathan's arm next to the remote.

Agnes stayed in the doorway. "I suppose you'll be wanting something to eat then." It wasn't a question. Her mother's dark eyes looked Mel up and down, inspecting, scrutinizing in the same way that had always driven Mel crazy. "I see you've taken off some weight. Looks good on you. Now if you'd just let your hair grow out." Her mother disappeared from the doorway leaving Mel to bite her tongue. Dropping thirty pounds as the result of chemotherapy for first stage breast cancer wasn't her preferred method of weight loss. She knew exactly how she looked: haggard, bones emerging from her body like knobby sticks with precious little flesh attached. But the doctors thought she had beaten it, so that was all that mattered. That—and the fact that the illness had drawn Calli closer to her. After all the horrors of the last year's treatments, it was clear Calli was hers for life and vice versa.

She met her father's eyes and he grinned up at her. "Guess you'd better go help your mother, Mel."

With a nod, she left the bedroom, wondering how her father, who was usually so kind to his daughters, had managed to stay with his wife for nearly forty years.

In the kitchen, Agnes, now clad in an apron over her pantsuit, was all business. She kicked the fridge shut, her arms full of containers and jars. Arranging them on the counter, she said, "Did you prepare something for your father?"

"Who, me?"

"Yes, you." She opened a drawer and pulled out a mean-looking butcher knife.

"I only arrived a few minutes ago. I haven't even been in this room 'til now."

Agnes set down the knife and turned to point at the microwave. "Open that." Arms crossed over her chest, she set her face in the angry grimace Mel had come to know so well over the years.

She pulled on the door to the ten-year-old silver appliance, and it clunked open. She bent to look inside. "I think a hotdog or sausage died a very ugly death here."

Her mother snorted. "Do you think it would have been so hard for him to clean up afterwards?" She turned back to the counter and hacked away at a hunk of salami three-inches in diameter.

Mel slid the plastic garbage container across the floor and used two paper towels to scrape out the mangled hotdog remains. She dampened the towel and wiped out the interior, then closed the door and returned the can to its regular space.

She heard a swishing sound as her father came up behind her in stocking feet. A second later, the click-click-click of toenails on linoleum announced Pete's entrance.

The bottom of a glass jar smacked against the counter. "Nathan, why on God's green earth can't you tidy up after yourself?"

Her father frowned. "Now what are you blatting about?"

Agnes pointed at the microwave. "If you're going to make hotdogs, you have to pierce them so they don't blow up all over the place. And when they do explode, kindly consider cleaning up afterwards."

"Hotdogs? What are you talking about? I didn't monkey with any hotdogs." His rheumy blue eyes came to rest on Mel. "Ask your daughter about this, Aggie. She looks like the guilty party to me!" He pivoted and stomped out of the room in a huff.

Agnes turned back to the sandwiches on the counter. Mel waited for some comment, some response. When one didn't come, she said, "Mom, what's going on with him? And I told you I haven't been in the kitchen."

With a sigh, her mother wheeled around and crossed her arms in front of her. "I know, I know. *He's* the one with the mustard stain down the front of his shirt, not you. I'm sure I'll have a dandy time trying to get that out." She paused as if debating her words. "The doctor says he has some memory loss due to mini-strokes."

"What?"

"For goodness sake, don't blame me, Imelda. He's old. He's seventy-nine now. This sort of thing happens."

"I wasn't blaming you. I just didn't know." Mel's hands went cold, and she felt shaky, as though she wasn't getting enough air. "When—when did this happen?"

"How should I know? It just did." Agnes opened the cupboard door, took down three plates, and stacked a sandwich on each.

"But, but—strokes? Plural? How many strokes?"

Agnes ignored the question, instead handing her daughter a sandwich on a plate and a bowl of potato salad with a silver spoon sticking out of it. "Here. Go sit down and eat."

Mel did as she was told, using the opportunity to take the deep, calming breaths a counselor had taught her in the past. Two bites of the peppery potato salad anchored her, made her feel solid again, but she watched her mother, waiting, knowing that Agnes had heard her question. She picked up the sandwich. The small bite of salami and cheese on rye went dry in her mouth, and unexpectedly, her eyes filled with tears.

Agnes moved through the room, skirting the breakfast table where Mel sat, and disappeared down the hall. A moment later her parents returned to the kitchen, her father first and her mother nagging at him from behind.

"I do *not* need slippers," Nathan said.

"But the A/C is cranked up high."

"It's goddamn summer out! I'm not an old man who can't make decisions, Aggie."

"I was just asking if you wanted any. I didn't mean a damn thing by it."

"Hmpph!" He jerked the chair away from the table and planted his behind in it. The expression on his face was so petulant that Mel suddenly choked out a laugh, which she quickly repressed. *Oh, no.* She closed her eyes for a few seconds, realizing that she was back on the merry-go-round again, one minute feeling teary, the next slightly hysterical. *How do they do this to me?*

Her father looked down at the plate and bowl before him, and in an instant broke out in a smile. "Well, look here, my favorite! Tuna and cheese." He picked up half of the sandwich, took a bite, and grinned again. "Excellent, Aggie. Just excellent."

Agnes stood, one hand on the hip of her dark blue pantsuit. "That's salami and cheese."

Mouth full, he looked up at her in amazement. Between chomps, he said, "Of course it is. What do you take me for—a moron?" He glanced at Mel, then back to his wife. "Oh, boy, you two are in rare form today. What did you have? Another fight?"

Mel met her mother's eyes, and for the first time in years, her mother's face showed helplessness. Anger, too, but also a silent plea for help. Before Mel could respond, the expression was gone, replaced by a narrowing of eyes and a sharp retort. As Agnes berated her husband, Mel blocked out the volley of harsh words and tried to calm her rapidly beating heart. Looking down at the cheery, plastic table cover, all pink fuchsia and deep purple violets on a white background, she realized she felt thirteen again. In the past three years—ever since Calli came into her life—she thought she'd progressed so much, and now here she was once again, sitting like a wooden horse in the kitchen as her father and mother exchanged insults. Horses up, horses down, 'round and 'round, never reaching any sort of destination. From experience, she knew the merry-go-round would slow for a while, but inevitably, it would resume. Sooner or later the bizarre tune always returned.

"What's that damn noise?" Nathan hollered.

Mel's head came up fast as she heard the same jarring chime. She rose smoothly and hustled through the kitchen, to the short hallway, and out to the living room where she pulled open her mini-daypack and grabbed her phone. "Yes?"

"Mel, honey, it's me."

"Calli." She let out a sigh of relief.

There was silence on the phone for a couple seconds. "Mel? What's the matter? Where are you?"

"I'm at my parents' place."

She heard a warm chuckle. "You must be a glutton for punishment. My parents last Sunday, now yours."

Mel looked around the living room, then lowered herself to the rose-colored couch. It made a whooshing sound as she sank into it, and though she couldn't see any dust, she felt a tickle in her nose and thought she'd sneeze. She said, "I thought you were painting today," as she rubbed her nose.

"Quick job after all. We just wrapped it up, and I'm off for the rest of the day. I got home, took a shower, and thought I'd call and check on you."

"Good idea."

"I get the impression that you can't say much, hmm?" Mel could tell Calli was smiling.

"Bingo."

"The only thing you really need to know, hon, is that the doctor's office called, and they need to reschedule tomorrow's blood draws. They can get you in today at 3:30 or else you have to wait until a week from Friday."

"Imelda?" Agnes stood in the doorway.

Mel wondered if her mother's x-ray eyes were scanning her slacks and blouse to see if any harm would come to the davenport. "Calli, will you give them a quick buzz for me and tell them I can come by for the blood draws today?"

"Sure."

"I'll be home right after."

"Okay, love. See you in a bit. Try to get out of there with your humor intact, and I'll take you to the movies tonight."

"Deal." Mel met her mother's eyes, and frowned.

Calli said, "Love you."

"Mmm hmmm . . ." Mel disconnected with the sound of Calli's purring laugh in her ear, and it gave her heart. "I've got to go, Mom." She hoisted herself up from the depths of the davenport and glanced back at it, thinking it was, after all, an engulfing, uncomfortable monstrosity.

"Wait a minute. What blood draws?"

Mel looked down toward her left breast, then looked away quickly. "Just another check for the—"

"Oh, I see." Her mother's voice was high and fast as Mel bent and dropped her cell phone in her bag. "Sure is lucky these days how they can excise the little problems so easily. Not like in the early days when that disorder was so dangerous to women."

"I'm not sure how much safer it is now, Mom. All I know is that chemotherapy is no fun."

"Well, dear, that's another thing you're lucky you didn't have to have." Mel's quick intake of breath caused her mother to pause and frown. "What? I'm no dummy, Imelda. Chemotherapy makes a woman go bald, and your hair looks fine, though you have always kept it too short."

Mel couldn't keep the look of disbelief from her face. The chemo she'd been through and the drugs for side effects hadn't caused much of her hair to fall out, but she'd gone through days of fever, vomiting and chills. Obviously her mother had not been paying attention, nor had she been listening to Izzy's progress reports. Mel scooped up her bag, stepped away from the rocking chair, head down, and made for the door.

"You want me to wrap up the rest of the lunch?"

"No, thanks, Mom. Let Dad have it. He seemed pretty hungry."

"It's probably better that you don't eat all that salami anyway. Too fatty, and now that you've finally got your figure where you want it, you don't want to run to seed." Agnes came close enough to reach out and touch Mel on the chin with a blue-veined finger. Her hand dropped away as she said, "You and your sister look so different. If only I had known. Look at those cheek bones, that nose, the eyes . . . maybe I should have named *you* after Isadora Duncan."

"Might have been a good idea, Mom. I'm never going to be the saint Imelda was, and Izzy won't ever dance."

"Ha. As if you ever dance," her mother said coyly.

Mel made sure her face didn't betray a thing, but inside, she was shrieking, *Yes, I do dance, and I'm damn good at it!* She pulled the door open. "Will you tell Dad I said 'So long'?"

"Sure will."

Mel stumbled to her car, thinking about names, and dying, and Catholic saints. In the year 1333, a day before Saint Imelda Lambertini's eleventh birthday, the little girl saint had died. She received her first Holy Communion and immediately afterwards dropped over dead, reportedly filled with ecstasy and joy. Saint Imelda was Mel's mother's patron saint. It occurred to Mel now, as she drove away from her parents' merry-go-round house, that little Imelda had probably killed herself after a run-in with her mother.

Later in the afternoon Mel walked out of the doctor's office picking at the sticky tape holding down a piece of gauze in the inside crook of her left elbow. She'd never expected to become such a pin cushion. If the cops ever arrested her, she was sure they'd think she was a junkie and not the law-abiding owner of an art gallery in Lowertown St. Paul.

She wandered out into the hot parking lot, her mind full of thoughts about her mother's comments regarding her father's strokes. He didn't appear unhappy, and except for when his wife nagged at him, he seemed content. Yes, he was seventy-nine, but he looked just fine physically, though today he had been a bit bleary-eyed. His cataract surgery five years earlier had been successful, but Mel thought he might need the procedure again.

She got in her Honda Accord, started it up, and adjusted the air conditioning vents. The warm, humid air quickly cooled. With it blowing on her, she actually felt too cold and turned it down to low.

All the way home she worried about her father, and when she walked into the townhouse she shared with Calli, she felt tired and wrung out. She found Calli in the kitchen assembling a salad.

"Hiya, sweetie," Calli called out. "Thought we could have something to eat, then go see what's playing at The Lagoon." Mel stepped into the kitchen, and Calli wrapped her in her arms. "Bad visit, huh?"

Mel sighed and pressed her lips against Calli's soft neck. "Yeah. No fun at all."

The phone rang, and Mel let go to look at the caller I.D. "Hey, it's the Venture Capitalist." She picked up the phone and said, "Nate! What's happening? How are you, bro?"

Her brother's voice sounded guarded. "We're fine here, just fine." He cleared his throat. "I called to let you know that I just talked to Mom."

She leaned against the fridge and watched Calli set the table. "Oh, so she told you about the strokes?"

"Ah, well, yeah. That came up. Actually, she asked me to tell you that Dad had a little accident in the car today."

"What! I was just there at noon! Is he okay? What happened?"

"Slow down, Mel. He's fine."

"Is he in the hospital?" Her heart raced in her chest, and she was glad to be leaning against something.

"Nope. Home resting already. He wrapped the Buick around a tree. Lucky that old boat is so huge. He was on the way over to the market and must have had a dizzy spell. He ran up on the sidewalk and into a maple in someone's yard. Bumped his head a little, but he's fine."

Relief spread through her at the same time that she was struck by the circumstances. "So she called you in California to report this?"

"Yeah, sorry about that. She said the docs gave Dad some meds for pain that will make him sleepy. She wanted me to call you and Izzy to tell you what happened and ask you both to let them be. He can't see anyone right now, but he should be fine by tomorrow."

What a chickenshit thing to do. For a moment she thought she'd said it out loud. "Nate, thanks for calling. Sorry you had to do the dirty work."

"That's what big brothers are for, right?" She let out a mirthless chuckle. "I promised I'd call Izzy, too, so I'm going to let you go. The kids and Sheila say hi."

"Give them our love, too." They said goodbye and hung up.

Calli stood by the kitchen table, watching Mel with a quizzical look on her face. "What now?"

"Dad cracked up the car, and instead of Mom calling us to report this little fact, she called Nate to have him do it."

Calli shook her head. "Families. Can't live with 'em—can't kill 'em."

She strode over and put her arms around Mel, who tightened her hands into fists, then hugged back. "I am just so damn mad, Cal."

"I know," she said. "I know." Leaning away, she said, "Skip the movie?"

"Yup."

"I'll put the salads in the fridge and we can have them when we come back."

Even though Nate had phoned Mel before he called her twin, Izzy lived closer and arrived at their parents' home first. As Calli steered into the driveway, Mel saw Izzy disappear into the house.

"You staying here?" Mel asked.

Calli nodded and patted Mel's thigh. "You don't need another body in there for the inevitable showdown. I'll keep the car cool for you." She squeezed Mel's knee and made her jump. "Don't break a leg, sweetheart."

"If I do, it won't be mine that gets broken." Mel got out and shut the car door, thinking how she talked a good game, but knowing her mother could snap her in two with little more than a few choice words. She marched to the front of the house and let herself in, pausing a few steps into the living room. She heard whispered hisses in the kitchen, and after a moment, she could make sense of the words.

"He's fine," her mother said in a hoarse stage whisper.

"I'd like to see for myself, Mother."

"Isadora, I asked you not to run over here. He needs quiet and rest until tomorrow."

"Right. And thanks for the personal touch. Having Nate call long distance was swell of you."

Agnes responded, but Mel tuned it out. No way was she entering the kitchen now, not when Izzy was fighting the good fight. All through their youth, she had marveled at her sister's ability to meet their mother head on. Mel couldn't remember a single time she herself hadn't folded.

Moving across the room like a man walking the plank, she stopped in front of the fireplace.

On the mantel were four elaborate German steins, two to the left and two to the right of the nautical clock in the middle. For all the years of Mel's life, her mother had hated those steins, which Mel's father had brought into the marriage. Nathan Bauer missed active duty during World War II, but was stationed in Germany the year after the war ended. He always said the steins were the only souvenirs he'd bought, and he intended to keep them. "I may even take 'em with me to the grave," he once said in the midst of an argument over them.

The steins featured delicate hand-painted reliefs of German scenes: castles of Bavaria on one, dancers flanking a colorful crest on the second, and a beer wagon, Bavarian hat, and pretzel on the third. Mel reached for the fourth, which was her favorite. A three-dimensional swan was delicately carved and inset. The plumed tail feathers made up the handle on the left. A tiny cygnet nestled under the breast of the bird, and on the right, the swan's head was bent gracefully, making it easy to grasp the overlarge stein and drink from it. Not that anyone ever drank from the foot-tall pieces of art—except for Henry Altamont, who, unbeknownst to Izzy and Mel, had filled the swan stein with cheap Annie Greensprings wine. This was 1991, while Agnes and Nathan were away from Minnesota visiting a dying elderly relative, and Mel and Izzy had used the opportunity to throw a summer party.

Mel turned the stein around. The crack in the baby swan's wing was still there, though she and Izzy, in desperation, had glued it back on. She tried to remember how long they spent hoping and praying no one would notice the crack—or the spot in the carpet near the couch where they'd had to cut away some of the shag rug because Tyler Schmidt gave Henry Altamont a bloody nose in response to Henry's carelessness with what he called "that damn antique mug." Tyler's protectiveness had earned him Izzy's heart. Thirteen years, one extravagant wedding, and two kids later, they were still together. Mel hadn't heard from Henry since he'd graduated from high school and was lost to the romance of the California cocaine trade.

She set the stein back in its place, turned it so the crack wasn't noticeable, and wondered why her parents had never asked about the swan's injury. Certainly neither of them ever mentioned it if they had noticed. She wondered if she could confess now. What would they say? What would her father think? And how long would it be before her father forgot he had ever possessed the mugs?

Just then Izzy rounded the corner into the living room and stopped abruptly. "I didn't hear you come in, Mel." Her face was bright red. Mel looked beyond to see their mother standing in the doorway, with an equally angry face and her arms crossed tightly over her chest.

"Uh, hi, Mom."

"I see you can't follow simple directions any better than your sister."

"Nope. Guess it's genetic."

"Your father is just fine. Come back tomorrow if you like."

Mel nodded. With a huff, Izzy grabbed her forearm and pulled her across the room. Without even a goodbye, they slammed out, letting the screen door slap shut behind them.

Mel looked back. Agnes stood behind the dull gray screen. In a hoarse voice she called out, "Don't think I don't know about your guilty fascination with your father's steins, Imelda."

Izzy pushed her forward. "The hell with her! Get in your car. You and Calli meet me over at the Caribou Coffee on Grand." She flounced off to her car, leaving Mel to wondering how many years her mother had known about the swan cover-up.

The next time Mel approached her parents' house, she arrived with prearranged reinforcements. Izzy sat in the Honda's passenger seat, toying with her long, straight hair, and gabbing about Mikey and Ashlee. Calli had graciously agreed to watch Izzy's two kids while the twin sisters spent the morning visiting their parents to talk about plans for the future. It had been two days since their father's accident, and after considerable discussion, the two sisters formulated a plan to suggest that their folks sell the house and move into an assisted-living center.

"Okay," Izzy said as they turned on their parents' street, "we have to do this good cop/bad cop style."

"Right. I suppose you're the good cop, as usual."

Izzy laughed. "I'm older, so shouldn't I get to pick?"

"Ten minutes shouldn't make that much difference. Besides, I'm a crappy bad cop."

"All right. You be the good cop, and I'll try to be the hellion. If that doesn't work, one of us gives a signal, and we can switch roles."

As Mel pulled up to the curb in front of the weathered house, she saw a green blob on wheels down the street. Like an over-sized alien, it weaved toward them.

"Oh, geez!" Izzy said. She pointed, her finger almost touching the windshield. "It can't be!" She grabbed the door handle and hauled herself up and out.

The green figure drew closer. Mel exited the car, shaded her eyes, and squinted into the sun. She met her sister's gaze over the top of the car and shouted, "What in the hell is Mom thinking?"

They slammed their car doors and stood waiting as their father wheeled up. A black, curly-headed Pete nestled between Nathan's bright white t-shirt and a heavy, forest green work shirt which was buttoned only halfway up.

"Dad," Izzy said. "What do you think you're doing?"

He applied the pedal brakes on the one-speed Schwinn and gingerly stepped off to straddle the bike. With his right hand, he reached up to his chest and patted Pete. The poodle gazed upward with a look of rapture on his face as his pink tongue darted out and licked Nathan's chin.

"Hi, girls. You must have gotten my transmission."

Mel glanced at Izzy. "Transmission?"

"Yes, sirree," he said. "I asked one of the men to make contact. Little did I know that he would send it out in JN-25 code, but I always knew my girls were smart. The Imperial Navy has nothing on our forces." He looked down at Pete. "Glad you figured it out. That's how we'll win the war—smart civilians and officers like me getting it done."

Mel pointed at a dark purple lump on his forehead above his left eye. Bisected by an inch-long slice, the wound was held together by two butterfly bandages. "How's your head?"

"No problem. You don't think the Japs and Krauts could get to me, do you?"

"What?" Mel wanted to step over and feel his forehead to make sure he wasn't delirious.

He smiled. "Don't worry a bit. We've stepped up our security on base."

Izzy frowned. "Oh. I see. Well, Dad . . . hmmm." She glanced toward Mel again. "So, have you had any lunch—I mean, been to the mess hall lately?"

He leaned forward and whispered, "No. Afraid the sergeant will stick me with KP."

"Don't worry about that," Izzy said. "You know I outrank the sergeant."

He let out a guffaw. "Nice try. Not *this* sergeant!" He leaned the bicycle to the side and dragged his right leg over to dismount. The Schwinn nearly toppled, but Mel leapt forward and grabbed it while Izzy steadied their father.

Mel said, "I've got it, Dad. I'll put it away for you—return it to the Motor Pool, that is. You go on into the house."

He shuffled over to the curb, stepped up, and took slow, even steps toward the front door. Mel waited until he was out of ear-shot, then turned to her sister. "Wasn't dad a soldier after World War Two?"

Izzy rolled her eyes. "Yeah. And where did he get all that stuff about codes and the Imperial Navy? He didn't have anything to do with that in the forties. He was never even an officer. I'll bet he's been watching the History Channel."

Shaking her head, Mel rolled the bicycle up over the curb and to the driveway. The garage door was locked. Without a word, Izzy went to the front door and disappeared inside. A moment later the automatic door rumbled up. Mel put the bike away, went into the house, and paused at the front door to press the garage remote.

Izzy stood in the doorway to the kitchen listening to their mother's sharp voice.

". . . supposed to do? Handcuff him to the bed? I didn't even hear him leave."

Mel squeezed next to Izzy in the doorway and said, "Mom, that's the point. You can't just let him roam the neighborhood. Two days ago he's in a car accident. Today he's on that old bike. He could have fallen or been hit by a car."

"And hello to you, too, Imelda," Agnes said in a tight voice. She stood holding a wooden mixing spoon in her fist. A spotless white apron covered her tan housedress. An array of spices, flour, and sugar sat on the counter next to her Kitchen Aide mixer.

With a sigh, Izzy said, "Mel's right, Ma. You've either got to watch him closer or he needs to be placed somewhere where they'll supervise him twenty-four hours per day. We had an idea. We think you should consider an assisted-living complex."

Mel thought her mother was going to attack. For one brief moment, her eyes resembled the piercing black gaze possessed by the swooping red falcon out in the living room curio cabinet. Agnes smacked the wood spoon on the counter, then confronted her daughters, red-faced and angry. "You want to send him to a home then? Just farm him out? He's *fine* and I can take care of him."

Izzy stepped forward allowing Mel to relax against the frame of the door. "He's not fine, Ma. The strokes have done something to him. He thinks he's back in the war."

Agnes waved a hand and picked up the wooden spoon. "Pshaw! Foolish nonsense. So he gets a little confused. He's seventy-nine, for God's sake. That's no reason to send him to an old folks' home when I can take perfectly good care of him. We're doing fine."

Mel shook her head. "But Mom—"

Agnes released her full fury. "You don't come around here for months at a time, Imelda, and then when you do show up, you think you can just walk right in and tell me how to take care of your father? Don't you try to tell me what you think is best! You, who don't even *have* a husband." She took two steps forward, shaking the spoon. "You have no right. None!"

Mel stood up straight, her face flaming, but she forged on, forcing the words to come out. "You always have to make things like this into something about *me*, about my lifestyle. You just can't do that anymore, Mom. Calli has nothing to do with this problem, so leave her out of it."

Izzy raised a hand, but before she could speak, Agnes shouted, "I'm sixty-eight years old and have every right to make judgments for my life and your father's, too." She shook the spoon in the air. "When you have a husband, only then can you tell me you know what's best. You're just damn lucky we didn't disown you over your—your—oooh!" She spun away, facing the kitchen window over the sink.

Mel closed her eyes and let out a long sigh. With a flash of insight, she realized that no matter what she did, or said, or how she acted—or even if she begged—her mother was never going to accept her relationship with a woman. Certainly Agnes would ordinarily be polite, though distant, but when her back was against the wall, Calli would never be accepted like Izzy's Tyler was. In her heart, Mel had always known this, but staying away from her mother had allowed her to avoid confronting the fact. In the past, she would have left in a rage long before this point in the argument, but now she merely felt deflated. Tears squeezed out as she heard Izzy's next statement.

"You're being unnecessarily cruel, Ma. Mel's right. This isn't about her. It's about Dad and what's best for him."

It was clear Agnes wouldn't back down. She let out a gasp of exasperation and jammed the spoon into the silver bowl on the counter.

Izzy said, "Ma! I've got a husband. Are you going to listen to me or is that just an excuse you're using to hurt Mel?"

"Get out."

Izzy turned and met Mel's eyes. She said, "Ma, you can't—"

"I said get out!" Agnes didn't turn around, but it was clear to Mel that the conversation was over. She backed up into the living room, facing Izzy as her sister came through the doorway shaking her head in anger and frustration. Izzy gestured to the left, and Mel wiped her eyes on her sleeve as she followed her down the hall to their parents' room.

Nathan lay on his side, his green work shirt untucked, with Pete curled up next to his slumbering body. Mel stood there long enough to see their dad's chest rise and fall, then whispered, "At least he's got Pete." When Izzy nodded, Mel saw the tears in her eyes. "Let's just go, sis."

Mutely, Izzy nodded, and they left the house, back into the humid morning. The heat took what little energy Mel had left, and she couldn't help the tears that welled up. They got in the car and sat quietly for a moment before Mel started the car and turned on the A/C. "What a big mess." She crossed her arms over the top of the steering wheel and let her head drop against her forearms. The touch to her right shoulder was firm.

"Don't let her get to you. She doesn't mean it." Izzy sniffed and let out a sigh.

"Yes, she does." Mel's voice was muffled, but she went on. "What's wrong with her? How can she be like that?"

Izzy shrugged. "Maybe it was her childhood, something with her parents—hell, I don't know!"

"Me neither. She knows just how to get to me, and she never wastes an opportunity."

"Mel, listen to me. You aren't going to get what you need from her. You never have and you never will. Daddy always loved you best, and she always loved Nate the most. Look at the bright side. At least you were *somebody's* favorite."

Mel sat back against the hot upholstery and stared at Izzy. She gasped out, "That's not true."

Izzy smiled. "Sure it is. And that's why it's extra hard on you— because sooner or later we're going to lose Dad, and he's the one that has always gotten you through. Maybe he won't die for a while, but we're losing him still. And then we'll be stuck with our cranky, mean-spirited mother, and there'll be no buffer at all."

The tears came, and Mel couldn't stop them. "How can you be so matter-of-fact about this?" she choked out.

"That's my job as the older sister—to look at the bright side."

"There's no bright side in this mess. It's a disaster all around. And what about you? Dad loved me, and Mom loved Nate best? You got screwed!"

Izzy shifted to the side in the awkward bucket seat and took Mel's face into her soft hands. "No, I didn't, little sister. I always knew *you* loved me best. That's the bright side."

Busybody

For eight years, Pearl and I have lived in Hobart, Minnesota, in one of the three apartments above a dance studio, which was formerly a dress shop. It was a lot nicer in the old days when the place downstairs was a dress shop open regular hours and with no late-night business except during the Crazy Days sidewalk sales every June. But ever since this goofball dance studio came in, there's been an endless stream of young ones shuffling in and out, loud music playing, and bumping and thumping until the ten o'clock news. Pearl and I learned to ignore the ruckus, and it doesn't hurt that our hearing isn't what it used to be.

Within three blocks, there's a butcher shop, grocery store and mini-mart, a bakery, bank, and drugstore. Just a little further up there's a bookstore, video rental place, and eight different restaurants—from Taco John's to Perkins. During winter, the streets are plowed quickly, and the area merchants keep the sidewalks sanded and salted. Pearl and I have always liked this little Minnesota town . . . except for the busybodies.

My mother and her friend Pearl have lived in Hobart, 65 miles south of the Twin Cities, since they retired. I know it's a long trip to visit me and Richard and the kids, but they have never complained. Lately I've been worrying about what would happen if Mom fell ill or was unable to drive. Would she come stay with us? And what to do about Pearl? She's like a second mother to me. She was there for Mom and me and the whole family when Dad died thirty years ago. But could we take in two elderly women? I just don't know.

I usually try not to think of Mom and Pearl being in their declining years, and in fact, I had managed to put it out of my mind completely—until they disappeared Friday night. Just vanished off the face of the earth: two seventy-three-year-old ladies—one with blue hair, the other with very little hair—driving a 1968 Bonneville. Rich and I didn't even know about it until the police called us Saturday, which was yesterday. Apparently, Mom's neighbor, Mrs. Olsson, saw the two of them get in their car in front of the dance studio with a man Mrs. Olsson described as "mean and scowly-looking." When Mom and Pearl didn't return Friday night or yesterday morning, Mrs. Olsson called the police.

The police haven't been able to find a trace of them, and we have no idea where they are. I've been worried sick. There's an all-points bulletin out for them covering the Midwest, and we gave the TV people their pictures to broadcast on the evening news.

Hobart City Courier, Monday, February 8th

Two elderly women, Pearl Jenkins, 73, and Alice Chisholm, also 73, have been missing from their Main Street Hobart apartment since Friday morning. Ms. Jenkins, a former St. Paul elementary school teacher, is five foot three inches tall, brown-eyed, with rinsed white hair. She was last seen wearing a light blue pantsuit, dark blue coat, white hat, and blue ski gloves.

Ms. Chisholm, a widow and the mother of two Twin City residents, is five foot six inches tall, brown-eyed, with short silver hair. She was last seen wearing blue jeans, white tennis shoes, a long black coat, red-and-white mittens, and a matching stocking cap. The two women were last seen traveling north from Hobart in a cream-colored 1968 four-door Pontiac Bonneville,

Minnesota license number WA992A. They were reportedly in the company of a tall, dark-haired man wearing faded blue jeans and a brown leather jacket.

Any information regarding the whereabouts of the two women, the identity of the man they were reported to be with, or the location of their automobile should be reported to the Hobart Police.

Oh, good grief! Here we are, Pearl and me—and three dozen other couples—at the Stone Ridge Lesbian Center and Commune in Illinois, when Christine, the woman who owns the place, comes running up to say Pearl and I are the subjects of a search party. Seems we're lost, wandered away, kidnapped, or the "victims of foul play." Christine heard it on the radio.

I could just kill that old busybody Neva Olsson. Things were fine until she moved in last fall. A spy! She's nothing more than a spy. Mean-spirited, nosy, opinionated, and downright rude. Why, just last week in the elevator, she said that women talk show hosts are no good and she only ever trusted Johnny Carson. She said Opera (that's what she calls Oprah Winfrey) was a crank who pried into other people's business. Neva should talk! She needs to keep her mouth shut, her binoculars in the drawer, and her curtains closed.

Pearl and I have been coming to this commune at least once a year since it started in 1969. Back then, Pearl and I had only been together about five years, and we needed somewhere comfortable and freeing to be ourselves, if only for one time during the year. We looked forward to it so much, and sometimes we've stayed two or three weeks. As we got older, we kept coming, and have made friends from all over the States and Canada. Some of the women write to us and visit during the year, and then we all rendezvous at Stone Ridge whenever we can. It's gotten to the point where we have had lots of input into the programs. Last year, we focused on Issues of Difference in the Lesbian Comm-unity. It's been enlightening to learn about transgendered men becoming women and about Socio-Economic Differences, Size-ism, and especially the Butch-Femme Continuum. I had never given much consideration to a lot of these topics. I may be seventy-three, but I'm still learning.

Usually in the winter, though, we come for a weekend retreat and serve as mentors to other young couples on their first visit. That's what we did all weekend, and we were going to hang around here until Tuesday morning. Now I suppose we have to go home. I should have told my daughter about this little jaunt, but who would have guessed that wretched busybody would cause such a stink? Curses on stupid, dim-witted Neva Olsson!

It's been over seventy-two hours since Mom and Pearl have been missing, and now the police may call in the FBI because it appears the man who was with them on Friday morning, Jeff Smith, was identified and picked up in eastern Wisconsin. He claimed that he knew Pearl from around town, and he'd hitched a ride with Mom and Pearl from Hobart. Why in the world would they be going to Wisconsin? The weather is cold, and it could snow.

Now I'm really worried. The man is in custody, and the police in Minnesota say the Wisconsin cops will eventually get the truth out of him.

If this awful man has done something to Mom or Pearl, I'll never forgive myself for not keeping a closer eye on them. God, I pray they're all right! If they're found safe and sound, I promise you, God, I'll never take my eyes off Mom again. She can move in here and have the sewing room. I'll take care of her like I never have before. Her life will be secure and happy. Oh, please God!

Hobart City Courier, Wednesday, February 10

Two elderly women previously reported missing from their Hobart apartment on Friday morning were found unharmed as they drove across the Minnesota border from Prescott, Wisconsin. Pearl Jenkins, 73, and Alice Chisholm, also 73, said they had intended to take an overnight drive into Wisconsin dairy country when Ms. Jenkins fell ill with the flu. The pair stopped for two nights at a motel until Ms. Jenkins recovered, then returned to Minnesota.

Neither woman could remember the name of the motel at which they stayed. When asked about Jeff Smith, the man with whom they were last seen in Hobart, they indicated that he is an acquaintance who had accepted a ride from them to a small town in Wisconsin.

Alice Chisholm was reunited with her daughter, Kathy Cross, and her three grandchildren. In an emotional statement, Mrs. Cross thanked the police and State Patrol for their assistance in locating her mother.

It just goes from bad to worse. Not only are Pearl and I under constant surveillance from that nosy old bat, Neva, but for the last two months, Kathy and her husband have been running down here at every opportunity to check on us, take us shopping, and keep an eye on us.

I'm choking!

I'm seventy-three-years-old, and I have to have a heart-to-heart talk with my own daughter. If Pearl and I want to live our own lives the way we always have, then I don't think we have a choice. Hell! I feel like a teenager trying to explain an all-night party.

So, Pearl and I are going over there tonight because we've decided it's time to open up the apartment, open up the doors, open up the closets—time for mother to emerge.

I'll never find my mother boring, that's for sure. Does she think Rich and I are dummies? Of course we know about her and Pearl. I've been sharing Thanksgiving and Easter and Halloween and Christmas and every other minor holiday with the two of them for over thirty years. Does she think I'm stupid—or blind?

It's the body language. There's no bubble around them. See, Mom and Pearl are so comfortable with each other, even more so than me and Mom—or Rich and me for that matter. Anybody halfway observant could tell.

Funny how nervous she was when she started her "confession." I let her go on for a while, then cut in and told her I've always known and that we didn't give a hoot. Mom isn't speechless too often, but she was pretty amazed for a couple minutes. And you should have heard Pearl laugh. I thought she'd spit her dentures across the room, she was laughing so hard. Then we all sat around and hugged and joked and ate steak and chicken that Rich barbecued on the grill.

So, nothing has changed. They don't want to move in here—together or apart—and I guess that's fine. They've got their lives to live, and I respect that. But I told them both, from now on, I get to have final approval of their itinerary. I don't want a repeat performance of this latest fiasco.

I woke up this morning thinking *one down, one to go*. It's time to go tell off that nosy old bat, Neva Olssen. Pearl kept telling me to let it all go, to forget about it, but I can't. If I can have the heart-to-heart talk with Kathy, then I think I can have the much-needed knock-down-drag-out with our busybody neighbor.

So I waited until Pearl settled down for a nap, and I went down to the other end of the hall and knocked on our nosy neighbor's door. Took her forever to answer, and I stood there thinking that I really didn't know this Neva Olsson at all, though she had lived in the building for several months. We had only run into her in passing, and I had always made an effort to be polite, but the hell with that noise now! I decided I would give her a piece of my mind.

The door opened slowly, and the tiny, silver-haired woman looked up at me. I had never paid attention to how small she is, but I felt like an Amazon giant, some sort of Xena, Warrior Princess, compared to her less-than-five-foot-tall stature.

"Oh, thank God," she said, relief in her voice. "I was so worried about you."

Well. That certainly took the wind out of my sails. I took a deep breath. "Yes, we're fine. What did you expect?" I know it came out a bit harsher than I intended, but then I reminded myself that I intended to be mighty harsh. Her eyes widened and I saw her swallow. I noticed then that she wore a loose dressing gown and slippers. Her face was flushed, and she held a tissue in one hand. In a kinder voice, I said, "I'm sorry. You're not well."

"No. I've had a bad cold."

"I won't keep you then."

I stepped back, but she hastily said, "No. No, wait." She opened the door wider. "Please. Come in for a moment."

At that point, I wished I had brought my mate along, suddenly thinking Pearl might handle the confrontation better than I would, but Neva was already turning, saying, "Have a seat, why don't you? I know your name is Alice, but we've never really talked."

I followed her a few steps into the foyer, then around the corner into a large airy room, similar to our own living room in size and window layout. The similarities stopped there. There was nothing quaint and homey about this living room. She owned a snazzy-looking davenport, matching love seat, and a bentwood rocker, but everything else was about as far as you can get from parlor material. Large animals, carved from wood, sat in corners and next to tables that held more carved animals, multi-colored rocks, and chunks of formed glass. To my right, near the love seat, sat a four-foot-tall wooden giraffe, complete with patches of dark brown spots burned into its coat and neck. A highly polished, chunky turtle made of some sort of shiny gray-green rock squatted on the floor under a glass table in front of the couch. Everywhere I looked, figurines, animals, and carved trees and flowers adorned the tables and floors. I wondered who in the world dusted them all.

But that wasn't the most startling aspect of the room. What took me aback most were the multitudes of photographs gracing every square foot of wall space starting about three feet off the floor and going up to within about a foot of the ceiling. The smallest were five-by-seven-inches, some were fifteen-by-twenty-inches, and others were the size of small posters.

I couldn't take it all in. Each photograph required more than just a brief glance. The one to my right displayed the wrinkled face of a sari-clad woman holding a tall cane with multi-colored ribbons hanging from it. Next to that was a desert scene with sand swirling in a tiny, little funnel cloud near a strange-looking red bush, the likes of which I had never seen. Some pictures were landscapes, some faces, some crowds of people or cityscapes. All were vibrant and amazing. That was the only word I could come up with—amazing.

Neva still stood in the middle of the room, looking back at me and sniffling. I know I was frowning when I met her gaze. "Did you take all these photos?"

She shook her head. She put her hand to her mouth and burst into tears.

I didn't know what to say—or what to do. I wanted to run. It's not like Pearl and I don't cry, but it doesn't happen very often, and surely not in front of strangers. The tiny woman backed up and lowered herself into the loveseat. She blew her nose into the tissue. I said, "I probably should go. I'm sorry to intrude."

She shook her head vigorously. "No, you don't have to go. I'm sorry. I'm just still so emotional. It hasn't even been six months since she died."

I cleared my throat. "Uh, what? Who? Who died?"

She waved her hand. "Come in. Sit down for a few minutes." I took three more steps and settled into the rocking chair. She went on. "We were together forty-seven years. I followed her everywhere." She teared up again. "But this is one place I can't follow—at least not quite yet."

I didn't know what to say, but I wanted to know who she was talking about. "What was her name?"

"Claire—Claire Neale Sutton, actually."

And then I understood. Claire Neale Sutton, the world-famous photographer from the latter decades of the 20th Century, the woman who documented the lives of women and children across the globe. I'd seen her photographs in newspapers and magazines for years, but not lately. I hadn't seen any for a number of years, though I couldn't put my finger on when they stopped. She had been a favorite of mine for years, and in fact, we even own a giant coffee table book of her work. "I have always admired her work, Neva. What happened to her?" I tried to ask as politely as possible, but my question brought on a fresh spate of tears.

"She died in my arms—a peaceful death. I woke up one morning and she was—she was gone."

Oh, my. I know I can be dense, but it didn't all come together until just then. Claire and Neva were lovers. As my grandson would say, *Duh!* How dumb could I be? "You and she were partners for forty-seven years?"

Neva nodded. "She was forty-two when we met. I was thirty-four. I fell hard. Lucky for me I came from money. In the 1950s, most women wouldn't have been able to afford what I could. It allowed me to follow her from site to site, to let her get to know me. She was a solitary woman, but I was persistent. It took three years, but after a time, she loved me, too. She needed me."

I watched Neva as her face brightened. The light in her eyes, which had seemed absent a few moments earlier, returned. She pulled a blanket over her lap and curled into the corner of the loveseat. I took a deep breath. "I bet you have a lot of stories you could tell."

"Oh, yes, Alice, I certainly do."

"You spent over five decades with her." Neva nodded at me. "And now you have moved here, to Hobart."

"Yes."

"Why Hobart?"

"Those were her wishes. This is where she was born. She's buried out in the Hobart Cemetery next to her parents."

I thought that was odd. Claire Neale Sutton traveled the world over. I would have thought she'd be buried in a Chinese province or Morocco or next to the Rio de Janeiro river—somewhere exotic—not here in small town Minnesota. I must have looked puzzled because she frowned. "She also thought I needed some place peaceful. But actually, I don't. I never did. However, I won't leave her." She lowered her eyes. "Even in death, I need her to know I am nearby, that I won't ever leave her. And when I die, I'll be cremated, and my ashes buried in her gravesite."

This brought on a fresh wave of tears, and I found myself wondering why this old lady, a woman who I had thought was a terrible busybody, was telling me all this. Again, I didn't know what to say, and all I really wanted to do was flee. But she looked up just then and lifted her chin in such a way that I suddenly could tell she was stronger than I thought. And I felt her loss. If Pearl were to die—and who am I kidding since one of us will, sooner or later—I would be devastated. Could I get over the loss in six months? Hell, no.

I studied Neva Olsson, and I knew. I knew what she would say next.

"I haven't known how to reach out, Alice. To make friends. Claire and I traveled all over, from continent to continent, never staying anywhere long. Two months here, six weeks there. We made friends everywhere we went, but with the understanding that it was all temporary. I never much minded. I had Claire. But now."

Her voice trailed off, and with a sinking feeling, I realized my error. All these months, this woman had been trying to reach out to Pearl and me, and I never saw it. I had assumed she was an old widow busybody—and actually, she is—a widow, I mean. But I had rebuffed her interest in us, thinking she wouldn't accept us, when, in fact, she wasn't so very different from Pearl and me after all.

Abruptly, I stood. In a blink of an eye, she seemed to sink into the couch, obviously expecting that I was rejecting her yet again. Instead, I said, "I know you aren't feeling well now, but when you've recovered, would you like to come to dinner at Pearl's and my apartment?"

Her face reflected surprise, then a relieved smile. "Yes, I would like that very much."

"And maybe in a few days Pearl and I could come back, and we could tackle the stories behind some of these photos and artifacts."

"Oh, yes! I have some amazing tales to tell, Alice."

I nodded. "I bet you do. And I suspect we probably have some to share with you, too."

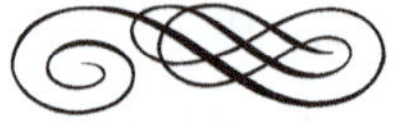

Propane

Tears escape and gush down Della's cheeks. She presses a terrycloth towel against her closed eyes, then uses it to blot her bloodied lip.

She opens her eyes and looks at the towel, lets it drop into the kitchen sink, not caring that the blood will stain the cloth. Her fingertips trace the red, ragged edge of a half-inch scar above her right eyebrow. It occurs to her that she is no longer healing from one fight before another happens. Softly, to herself, she says, "That's the last time. She's never gonna hit me again."

Through the frosty pane over the sink, she sees her lover Kerry stomping around the snowy backyard. The tall woman carries a shiny red can in her left hand. With her right leg, Kerry kicks repeatedly at a huge pile of old branches and brush, which she has made into a haystack mound six feet tall. After each round of enraged kicks, she stops to point a stream of liquid from the can until it is empty. After shaking the last drips from the can, she tosses it aside and fumbles in her jacket pocket.

Della looks down at the broken plates on the floor. They were a moving-in-together present from Kerry last year. Seven of the plates from the eight-place setting are now broken. They crunch beneath her feet. She bends over to pick up the large, jagged pieces and throws them toward the garbage pail. One piece hits the wall and shatters before falling into the pail. Della sweeps up the smaller shards.

Broom and dustpan in hand, she looks out the window again and sees a blaze of fire leaping skyward. *It's over*, she thinks. *I'm moving out.* More tears course down her face, and the salt-water stings when it reaches her cut lip. She wipes her face on her shirtsleeve and peers out to watch Kerry heave more branches on the blazing brush pile. Before any thought registers, an odd tremor of electricity runs up her spine. At the same instant, Della sees a silver line shoot from the flaming woodpile toward the red can. As Kerry steps away from the fire, a flashing blast of gold and pale purple strikes her in the thigh. She is engulfed in flame and falls face down into the newfallen snow.

Della doesn't breathe. Doesn't move. Her mouth opens, but she makes no sound. Kerry gets up on her knees, arms outstretched. Flames and black smoke swirl around her. Della hears Kerry scream, a loud piercing sound she has never before heard from this woman. Her jacket and pants are aflame, and even her hair is on fire. Della drops the broom and dustpan. She grabs the bloodied terrycloth towel from the sink. Rushing from the kitchen, she wrenches open the sliding glass door, screaming her lover's name.

A mass of smoke and blaze, Kerry is on her feet, stumbling away from the bonfire.

"Stop!" Della shouts. "Please, Kerry. Stop!"

Kerry is slowed by the flames and her heavy boots, but still she slips and scrambles across the yard at a fast pace. Della has never run so fast. She pitches herself at Kerry, hits her at the knees, and drags her down.

"Roll, dammit! Roll!" She chokes and coughs as she beats furiously at her lover's body with the towel. Kerry pants and kicks and squirms. When she rolls to her right side to try to get up, Della shoves her facedown, straddles her hips, and uses the towel to put out the flames on her back. Still, fire licks the upper arms and collar of the ski jacket.

Rising to a crouch above her, Della says, "Help me, Kerry. Come on! Roll over for me." Her voice is raspy and desperate.

Kerry hefts her forearm and shoulder back and slides over onto her side. Kneeling next to her, Della wraps her hands in the dishtowel and beats at the last of the flames, then drops the seared terrycloth into the snow. She scoops clumps of snow onto Kerry's neck, face and shoulders. Kerry jerks and writhes until she lies on her back, smoldering and panting and wide-eyed. But there are no more flames. An acrid, scorched odor surrounds them. Della's head pounds, and she is sick to her stomach. She takes a huge breath and holds it until the wave of nausea passes.

"I'm okay," Kerry says. "It doesn't hurt."

Kerry looks up at her with her goofy, all-knowing smile, and Della has the impulse to strike her. Instead, she jumps up from her kneeling position and stumbles away. Kerry tries to rise, but falls back, her melted ski jacket making a crumpling and cracking noise. Della reaches out her hand to help, but Kerry is too heavy and has to turn over on her stomach without help, push herself up to her knees, and stagger unsteadily to her feet. Pale and glassy-eyed, she stands wavering in the bitter wind. Della puts a hand out to steady her.

"Guess I ruined a perfectly good coat." Kerry grins as she brushes her fingers over the chest. Bits of charred material flutter to the ground. "I had no idea that propanol-butane crap was so explosive."

"You—you—you—" In her fury, Della cannot think of words to say, and the blood rushing to her face feels almost as hot as the fire did.

Kerry glances toward the bonfire and does a double take. "Whoa! The brush is slipping down near the fence. I better—"

"No!" Della screams. "You're in shock. Get the hell in the house. I'll call 9-1-1."

Again Kerry smiles, shakes her head, laughs a little. "Calm down. I'm fine. Trust me. I just look like shit is all."

Della scowls at her, then runs through the snow, slipping and nearly falling. In the house she calls an ambulance. When she hangs up the phone, she notices that her hands and forearms are crusted with soot. She scrubs them clean at the sink with green Palmolive liquid soap. There are no dishtowels to dry her hands, so she wipes them on two paper towels. Her lip is still throbbing, and when she touches a damp paper towel to it, the light pressure splits it open. Again, she tastes the salty, bitter blood.

Through the window she watches Kerry moving around the fire, poking at it with a long stick. The brush settles, and the flaming branches writhe and curl, sinking into the center of a red and gold furnace. The twisted and gnarled lump of the now-blackened red can rests in the snow nearby.

Kerry turns away from the fire, strides slowly toward the house, and raises a hand when she sees Della staring at her through the window. Her clothing gives off steam and tiny curls of black smoke. She slides open the patio door and steps inside, stands next to the dining room table.

Kerry's hands, her ears, and the sides of her neck are red and blistered. Her eyebrows are gone, and so is much of her short reddish hair, replaced by sooty white spots and charred gray patches of scalp. Della kneels before the big woman and unlaces her Sorel snow boots. Kerry leans heavily, pressing down on Della's shoulder as she steps out of the boots. Della notices a jagged gash in Kerry's jeans and sees blood oozing from her lover's thigh.

She rises and runs down the hall to the linen closet, grabs a stack of folded blankets, and rushes into the living room.

"Get in here," she shouts as she drapes a blanket over an easy chair.

She frowns as Kerry shuffles toward her. Della takes her by the arm, pulls her in front of the easy chair. "Wait. Take off your pants first." Kerry reaches down and fumbles with the Levi buttons as Della struggles to unzip the ski jacket. At first, it will not separate from the shirt beneath and she fears it's welded to Kerry's body. Then the material loosens and peels off in strips.

Della hears a siren, a mosquito whining far away. It grows louder, decibel by decibel, while she gets the charred pants off, removes as much of Kerry's melted jacket as she can, and then pushes her into the chair and wraps her in the other two blankets. Kerry's face is ashen, her eyes vacant. She squints, as if she is trying to see something far away. Her breathing quickens.

"Della," she pants. "Something's wrong. Oh, Jesus. It hurts really really bad." Kerry cradles her head, wincing, and says, "Oh, Jesus. Oh, Jesus . . ."

Della lets herself fall into the other easy chair. She closes her eyes and tries to think what to do next. Nothing comes to mind. *It's not my fault*, she thinks, *not my fault. What could I have done?*

The ambulance enters the driveway. Footsteps pound on the stairs, and Della jerks to attention. She jumps up to open the door. Three paramedics cluster around Kerry and spread open the blankets. One gets out syringes and bottles and instruments. The red-haired woman is now moaning in pain. Della moves off to the side.

"I think she said it was propane," Della says. "It blew up in the back yard—burnt her bad."

Nobody pays any attention, and she realizes how obvious the accident must be to them. Of course, she's burned. The room stinks like scorched plastic and flesh, and the cloth still clinging to Kerry's torso and legs is crusty and blackened.

"Looks like second degree mostly, maybe some third," Della overhears one man say into a scratchy-sounding walkie-talkie.

A beefy paramedic, rumpled and sweating, taps Della on the shoulder as someone pulls a stretcher past her. "Ma'am," he says, "looks like you hurt your lip. Want me to take a look at it?"

She nods. She wants to tell him about the fire and the red can and her fight with Kerry, but her mind is in a jumble. All she can think is that he will not understand, no matter what she tells him. How could she make anyone understand what she herself does not?

The paramedic touches her lip with a latex-gloved finger and says, "That's pretty deep, but I don't think you'll need stitches." He shines a light into her eyes, nods, and tucks the silver penlight back in his jacket pocket. Reaching into his supply bag, he pulls out a package, rips it open, and puts a gauzy white compress to her lip. The stinging brings tears to her eyes again, and she takes a deep breath to calm herself.

As she watches two men secure Kerry to the stretcher, Della hears her growling against the pain. Again, the medic touches Della's arm. He asks, "Are you a relative?"

"No."

"Oh. Well, do you want to come with her in the ambulance anyway?"

She hesitates. A wave of fatigue washes over her, and all she wants to do is sit.

"Come on," he says. "Get a coat. You can call her family from the hospital."

"No," she says. "It's okay. I'll follow in the car." He shrugs and rejoins the other paramedics as they wheel Kerry through the front door and carry her down the stairs. The bitter cold Minnesota wind blasts through the open door. Della shudders, feeling frozen to the core. She closes the door. Through the window, she watches them load Kerry into the back of the ambulance, crawl in behind her, slam the door shut, and back down the drive.

She pulls her warmest winter coat from the hall closet, lifts her shoulder bag off the hook, and trudges out to the yard. As she waits for the automatic garage door to open, the ambulance gets a break in traffic and backs into the road, lights flashing, siren whining. She watches it go left, up and over the hill, speeding toward the center of the city. Though it disappears over the crest, she can still hear the fading siren as she gets in her car.

Della sits shaking for a moment. After the tears come and go once more, she wipes her eyes on her sleeve, starts the engine, and backs out. She taps the button to close the garage door and eases the car into the street. She turns right, away from the siren, away from all she has come to know. Pressing the accelerator to the floor, she heads away from the city, away from the pain, down the long, steep hill.

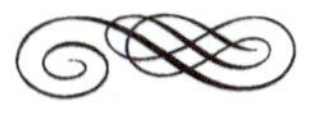

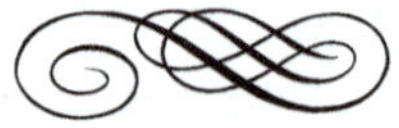

Vagabonds

It occurs me I may never wear a dress to a funeral again. I really mean it! You can forget pumps, too. I've always hated dresses and makeup and all that nonsense. Give me a nice, worn pair of jeans or sweat pants. I'll take those any day.

I own two dresses: one for funerals—appropriate dark blue with subtle white trim—and a splashy flowered number for weddings. Neither get-up is comfortable, so I try to avoid weddings and funerals like the plague. But that day, I suffered through in the dark blue dress because my friend Virginia had died. Who would have thought I'd want a fast get-away from her funeral? Believe me, I did; and the stupid dress was no help at all.

I went to the funeral home early to pay my respects. I didn't want to go one bit, but I made myself, even though I had to take time off from work. When my boss in the Food Stamp Department found out it was for a funeral, she let me go in an instant. In the last five years, seems like we've been rotating losses. First, my mother, then her sister. My aunt, her mother. My lover's father, her cousin. No one she knew had died since my uncle passed on last month, so this broke the chain, and I think she was grateful.

I bused from the downtown welfare department out to the funeral home. It wasn't a very nice spring day, but at least it wasn't raining, or I'd have been totally uncomfortable in my ridiculous dress and stupid, not-so-sensible heels.

Even though I hate funerals and detest eulogies, it seemed only right that I go to say goodbye. Besides, I figured there wouldn't be many people in attendance. Most of the gang from the old days had quit, moved on to better jobs, or ceased to have sympathy for a woman who couldn't take pressure on the job. Virginia Gallagher's cause of death wasn't mentioned in the obituary, but Mick, the deputy in the welfare lobby, knew what had happened. Virginia overdosed on drugs and alcohol over the weekend.

When I entered the funeral home—one of the few in the metro area I hadn't yet visited—I saw I was right: there weren't many mourners. In fact, I didn't see any mourning going on at all. In the foyer, I introduced myself to a short, balding man in a business suit who was standing by a couple of younger women who turned out to be Virginia's cousins. The man said his name was Peter, Virginia's uncle. Nodding politely as he turned away, I stepped through one of the double doors leading into the side of the chapel and saw a dim room with walls made of brick. Every ten feet or so dull light seeped in through the dusty windows. Between each window, fake-marble columns were glued to the wall to make it look like they were imbedded in the brick. Wooden benches pressed flush up against the wall and ran north to south. The casket was at the east end of the room.

At the front, but off to the side, stood two over-cologned men in fancy suits, hands clasped in front of their belt buckles. The faint smiles on their faces and the eyebrows raised in angelic sympathy told me right off that they were the funeral director and mortician. I walked past them to the front and joined three old ladies at the casket.

"Don't she look good?" one woman asked as she smoothed a wrinkle in her pale purple pantsuit.

"Oh, yes," the blue-haired one said. "Much better than last year when she came by my house wanting cash, supposedly for surgery on her cat. Hah! The way she staggered, I could tell she'd been drinking. Probably needed money for more booze. I sent her on her way."

"Now, now, we shouldn't speak ill of the dead," the third woman said. "Goodness! Her spirit could be floating right here, right now! I read about it in the *Enquirer*."

The three women glanced up, peering around at the walls and ceiling. I looked up, too, but all I could see were a few cobwebs hanging from the fake gilded columns.

As they turned and wobbled back to the pews, I heard one of them say, "Wonder what they're serving at the lunch today." I found myself hoping these ladies weren't related to Virginia, but if they were, I understood why she'd taken to drink

I tiptoed forward to the pressed-wood box and was horrified at the change in Virginia. Her hair was graying and clumpy, her complexion muddy, and paper-thin skin barely covered her bones. Someone had dressed her in the world's ugliest, tackiest, olive green polyester pantsuit, and they hadn't even put a blouse on under the jacket. She looked small and scrunched up, like she died in pain.

I stepped aside, pulled a huge wad of tissues from my purse, and snuffled my way back to one of the long pews. It was a small chapel, with only twelve or fourteen rows. I didn't want to sit too close to the front, and there was a man hunched over in the last pew who looked like a lost vagabond, so I opted to take a seat three rows from the back. I slid in and tried to catch my breath.

The man behind me slipped out of the back row and trudged up to the casket. He wore a bright white shirt, which looked all the more striking in contrast to his filthy, oily, blue-brown pants and crusted tennis shoes. His black hair was shaggy and unkempt, and he carried a ratty green rucksack in one hand. Stopping ten feet from the casket, he stood on his toes, head raised, leaning forward as if he were peeking over a cliff from as far a distance as he could get.

After a moment's hesitation, he shuffled forward, dropped the rucksack, and stood with his hands on the edge of the casket.

I blew my nose, tried to adjust my pantyhose without drawing attention to myself, and glanced at my watch. It was after two; time to get started. When I looked up at the front of the chapel, I was startled to see the man gesturing wildly at Virginia, hands rotating and flopping, then making quick grasps in the air as though he were trying to catch her attention one last time. I couldn't see his face, but I heard the rising and falling hum of his voice as he carried on his conversation. In an abrupt jerk, he stepped back, retrieved his rucksack, and turned around. His face was haggard, and as he drew near, I saw his sadness in the set of his jaw and squint of his eyes.

Just then, a priest and several other people came in from the foyer. They stood in the side aisle talking, laughing, coughing, and whispering loudly. The vagabond man stopped in front of them and said, "Hey! You ain't got no respect for the dead?"

Five people's mouths dropped open in concert as the man waved his free hand and spoke in a loud voice. "That's my ol' lady up there. My woman. Have some respect. Don't you people have any respect?" His voice cracked, and a strangled sound came out, then, softly, "She's my woman, don't you know?"

The priest stepped forward. Very softly, he said, "We're sorry, sir. We didn't know." With a nod toward the others, the priest said, "Let's all be seated now. I'm sure you must be ready to start." He turned and ushered the people into a pew up front, and then disappeared through the side door with the funeral director and mortician.

The man shook his head and looked as though he were going to cry. Actually, I thought he was going to leave. I *hoped* he was going to leave. He stood at the side for so long, first looking toward the pews, then toward the foyer, then back. When strains of creaky organ music began, he leaned forward, and took a step—toward me. He sat down in my pew. Glancing over at me nervously, he proceeded to slide his scrawny behind toward me one foot at a time. I tried to ignore him, but the acrid liquor smell he emitted made him hard to shrug off. I scooted toward the wall thinking I could give him more space, and he slid even closer to me.

He reached over and grabbed my sleeve. "Didja know her?" he asked as he breathed out such a wretched odor of rotting food and cheap liquor that I thought I'd faint. I hate bad smells. Virginia used to tease me because I didn't even like the smell of the ink on the food stamps.

"Yes," I told him in a hoarse whisper. "We used to work together."

"What? Come off it. She never worked."

"Sure she did. We worked down at the welfare building until about seven or eight years ago."

I explained to him how I met Virginia at the county welfare department nearly fifteen years ago. We were both just out of high school and went through the training program at the same time. I loved her sense of humor, and we laughed often over the reported antics of her large family of cats and dogs. We worked with three other women in the food stamp department—at the same glamorous job I still hold— trying to help those less fortunate. It was an easy job at first, until we got to know the clientele. Then they changed over time from "those less fortunate" into real, live people like Alvareen, who had unmanageable twin boys whose shenanigans got her regularly kicked out of apartments. Or Carolyn, the disabled flower vendor who kept getting mugged on her corner by passing skate-boarders. Or Nancy or Simon or Mike or Meltona, each struggling with MS or heart ailments or mental health problems. It got to be a hard job, watching all those folks trying to live on a shoestring.

I thought I was a sucker for a sad story, but Virginia was even worse. We weren't long at the job before she was bringing in doughnuts and cookies—not for us, for the clients.

"Sir," I said as I tugged my arm away from the man. "Could you let go of my sleeve?"

"Sorry. Sorry. Sorry." He spoke loudly and shook his head from side to side as though he were trying to shake something loose from it. "I'm just so damn upset. She died. She died. I wasn't even here, and she died."

"Did you know her long?" I whispered.

He turned surly. "Of course I knew her. Why the hell would I go out and steal a clean white shirt if I didn't know her?" Then his face crumpled up as if he were going to start bawling. Instead, he squinted, grimaced, and burst out, "You sure you knew Ginny? Prove it to me. Whaddya know about her?"

I wanted out. I looked around the chapel. I was pinned up next to the wall on my left, and the man blocked my way to the right. I gauged whether my dress would stretch far enough to allow me to vault the pew ahead, and I came to the conclusion it would not. The organist—the terribly bad organist—played loud enough to drown out most of the vagabond man's rambling, but not loud enough to cover the noise I would make flipping head first into the next pew. I was stuck.

"She was a real sweet girl," I said. "The thing I remember best was her love for animals." He leaned toward me and stared intently into my face, which made me very uncomfortable, but I went on. "I'll never forget one day coming in to work on Warner Road, and there was a terrible traffic tie-up. I figured it was an accident, but as I drew near the welfare building, I saw Virginia had pulled her VW Bug half off the road and was trying to lift a heavy dog she later told me had been grazed by a car. She sure loved cats and dogs and every living thing."

"Damn straight," he said, and he said it so loudly that the old ladies up a few rows inclined their heads to the side to try to listen. He fidgeted and his hands shook, then he stared at me, cracking his knuckles. I wracked my brain for some piece of information to calm him.

"Oh, yes. One time—I'll never forget this one—a bat got in and was dive-bombing the entire department. Every time a phone rang, the bat swooped down. Everybody was screaming and running. I remember two fat women trying to cram under the same desk."

I started to laugh. The man glared at me, but I couldn't stop laughing. "You don't understand," I said to him. "Sixty-five people had jammed under desks or stampeded with me to the elevator. And Virginia was the only calm one. She was trying to catch the bat in a small garbage can so she could set him free. She didn't want him to be hurt."

I could still remember the absorbed look on her face as she offered the wastebasket up with both hands, almost like a chalice. I don't even know what happened to the bat. I got one last glimpse of Virginia up on a desk, both hands cradling the container, and then the elevator door closed.

From the side door of the chapel, the funeral director and mortician slithered into the room, went to the front near the casket, and signaled to the organ player. The vampire music tapered off to a mere sixty decibel. Again, I felt tears come to my eyes. "You know how she was," I said as I turned back to the man. "Virginia couldn't stand to see anybody or anything hurt."

The man nodded at me, a solemn look in his tired eyes.

Virginia was not a judgmental person at all, which was something I loved about her. She didn't care how poor you were or what kind of home you came from. She didn't care a bit when I nervously confided to her that I had fallen in love—with a woman. "Love is good," she said. "Love is all that matters. Be happy! Live life! Have fun!" Then we both started laughing until the food stamp workers around us thought we'd gone crazy.

"Mister, I have to say Virginia was a woman full of love and caring for every being on the planet. She was just a lovely person."

He nodded again, and for a brief moment I thought he would finally drop his guard and let the tears come. Instead he bellowed, "She was a wonderful person, and believe me before I," his voice got even louder, "she didn't go for any of this Christian bullshit. She shouldn't even be in here!"

"Sir, sir," I said as I looked around at everyone staring back at us. The three older ladies were frowning and whispering amongst themselves. I know my face turned red. I patted the man's shoulder and tried to calm him down. "What's your name?"

"Otis. I'm Otis," he shouted. "Didn't she talk about me? You have to know who I am. I'm Otis, the only man she ever loved." His voice trailed off in a strangled sob. He opened his rucksack and rummaged around in the clothes and papers inside and pulled out a thick packet of letters lashed together with six or seven rubber bands.

"Look, look," he shouted. "These are the letters she wrote me when I was in treatment last month. See?" He thrust them at me.

"Oh, that's okay. I don't need to read the private letters she sent you. I understand. So *you're* Otis, of course. Of course." He stared at me for a moment, then stuffed the letters back in his rucksack, pulled the worn flap over it, and threaded three leather straps through like tiny little belts.

The horrendous organ solo ended, the final note wavering and fading as the priest strolled up to the lectern. The ladies continued to stare at us until the Father cleared his throat and the congregation of twelve gawkers turned to the front. The priest gave his opening remarks and then moved into a eulogy, but I guess it must have been in parables because I didn't understand how any of it related to Virginia. He talked about lying down in pastures and eyes in needles, and sisters and brethren, and I started wondering if I was having a bad dream. I tuned him out and focused on memories of Virginia and what a hard life she'd had.

After a few years at the welfare building, she started taking Valium, then drinking half the nights, and sneaking out on break to smoke pot under the railroad trestle that ran next to our building. People did the best they could to get her off the stuff. More than once we got a call in the morning from the Detox Center downstairs saying she had been found the previous night, passed out in some alley or back street.

For a long time, I covered for her. I'd tell the supervisor she'd called in sick, and sure enough, in a day or so Virginia would show up to work. She'd be a little shaky, her hair uncombed, and she often had burn marks on her fingers from falling asleep with a cigarette in her hand.

Eventually though, the boss got wise. None of us could keep up with Virginia's caseload and our own work, and complaints about her came in from the food stamp recipients. Then when we converted to a computerized system, management could tell she wasn't producing statistics. The high mucky-mucks sent her to treatment, not once, but twice. They gave her verbal reprimands, letters, warnings, a suspension, and then finally, they fired her.

For the last several years, I've seen her wandering around town, and there were lots of times when she was so deep in her own personal fog that I couldn't have gotten her attention if I had done cartwheels in her face.

Other times she recognized me right off and said, "Hey, Patty, old pal. How are ya? What's happening?" She'd wink and say, "So, how's Terese?"

If she was too smiley or glassy-eyed, I'd just pat her and say something soothing, then move on. If she wasn't too high, I'd tell her about vacations Terese and I were planning, or plays and movies we'd seen. I tried to treat her with respect, not letting on that I thought she was ruining her life, because I honestly had no idea what to do for her. I can't say I really understand the downward slide she took. She seemed okay until her parents began failing. Her mother had lupus, and her father's heart was weak. I knew they'd been in poor health ever since she was a little girl. With her being the only child, they depended on her for much of their care. The only help they'd ever been able to give her was a little money here and there. She once told me they lived on a trust fund.

After she was fired, I know Virginia moved back in with her parents, but then they both died. I don't know if it was devastating for her or a relief. I just lost track.

I was smacked out of my memories by the sound of the priest's hand pounding the lectern as he shouted something about being my brother's keeper. I wasn't sure how brothers related to Virginia, since she had none, but then I think the priest said she was a fugitive and a vagabond in the earth—which I felt was going too far! It's true that she was going to her final resting place in the earth, but she had been somebody, a person—a woman who had cared, and who was crushed into fine dust by the overload.

I considered how I hadn't been much of a friend to Virginia. How I hadn't thought to do one thing to really help her. How she never harmed anyone in her life, except herself. How I never really under-stood her even though I could see her pain. Yet I didn't do anything. Next thing I knew, I was crying good and hard, and Otis, smelling of whiskey and body odor, put his arm around my shoulder and said,

"Yeah, yeah. It's terrible. I don't believe it, either."

The priest finished his words of wisdom, and a silence fell over the chapel. A few rows up, the lady in the purple pantsuit leaned forward to the man ahead of her and asked him a question. I'm sure she thought she was whispering in the way that people do when their hearing has gone straight to hell, but Otis and I both heard her ask, quite clearly, "Peter, whatever happened to her trust funds?"

Otis stood up, and as he rose, he tossed his rucksack up into the air, nearly as high as the ceiling. It came down and splatted onto the bench ahead of us. His face turned red, and he began making a choking, gurgling noise. I pressed myself up next to the brick wall as he stood, ramrod straight, and shouted, "Ginny's dead, and nobody gives a shit. Nobody 'cept maybe this lady here." He pointed at me. "She's dead, and nobody cares. Nobody cared when she was alive, and now she's dead, you just want her money. Well, I got news for you. We took care of her money. Nobody's ever going to get it. We took care of it, took care of it good."

Tears coursed down his face as he leaned forward, picked up his rucksack, and turned to leave. I don't think anyone in the chapel was breathing; I know I wasn't. There was a simultaneous sigh of relief when he disappeared out the chapel door. People shifted and coughed, looking around as though nothing had happened.

From his seat in front of the purple pantsuit lady, Peter turned and said, "Ivy, in answer to your question, I don't know what happened to her trust funds. I disbursed the money to her last month and ended my duties as trustee."

Ivy, who had begun to rise, sat back, making a thumping noise. "Well," she said in what I'm sure she thought was her most nonchalant voice, "so how much was it, Peter?"

"I can't remember the exact figure. It was a few dollars over two hundred and thirty thousand."

It was silent for about three seconds, and then suddenly everyone in the chapel was on their feet. Ivy toddled toward me, face wide-eyed, lipstick askew. "Ma'am, ma'am! Your friend," she said as she waggled one arm in the air. "What's his name? Who was he?"

I shrugged my shoulders, shook my head, and gave her my best dumb look. She passed on by and headed toward the door. The organ player hit the first few notes of "What a Friend We Have in Jesus," and the funeral director stood at the front looking surprised. In seconds, everyone but Virginia and me had leapt up and rushed out the door shouting, "Hey, wait!" and "Where'd that guy go?"

Over the whine of the organ, I heard a shout and someone said, "He's gone! He disappeared!" Then the door shut behind them, and their scuffling and shouting faded away, leaving me sitting alone in the tacky little chapel.

I hoped Virginia and Otis took care of the trust money—maybe gave it to an animal rights group or to an animal shelter. She couldn't have spent all that money in one month, and it wasn't likely Otis got any of it or he wouldn't have had to steal the shirt he'd worn today.

I stood, smoothed out the wrinkles in the front of my dress, and walked up the aisle to the casket. The funeral director opened his mouth to say something, but I cut him off. "Just give me a moment, will you?"

He nodded and gave a broad smile, then retreated through the side door.

The organ din covered my final words as I stood over the still body of my old friend. "Goodbye, Virginia," I told her. I took one last look at her sad face. "I hope you've gone to a better place."

I turned and went out the chapel door. My fellow mourners clustered around one another gesturing, arguing, and complaining. I hurried past them in my uncomfortable blue high heels, past the manicured lawn of the funeral chapel, and down the street to the bus stop. *Run fast, Otis*, I thought to myself.

And I hoped with all my heart that Otis had disappeared for good.

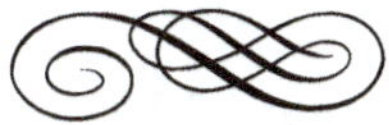

Afraid of the Dark

In Memory of the inspiration of Judy, Ruby, and Del
"All who wander are not lost . . . Usually?"

Marin sat hunched in the jouncy seat as the bus rumbled down the windy street, sucking in and spilling out riders. The bomber jacket on the young man seated ahead of her smelled leathery and musty, tickling her nose and making her sneeze. She looked away from the window and closed her eyes for a moment as the swaying and rolling of the warm bus made her sleepy and relaxed for the first time all day.

The bus rolled to its next stop, one block from her childhood home. Marin looked out the window again and saw sloppy snow, half rain and half ice, falling. She pulled a heavy satchel out from under her seat, waited to get off the bus, then stepped from its warmth into the chilled air. She walked swiftly around icy puddles and hunched against the biting wind.

As she strode up the long walk to her mother's two-story house, she noticed how cracked the walkway had become. Dead weeds and obstinate shoots of gray-green grass poked out through the chips and cracks. Her mother had stopped edging the walk, and the battered lawn was weedy and unkempt. She jumped when the screen door smacked open and hit the wrought iron railing. It bounced back halfway. Marin's mother, chunky in her quilted copper-colored coat, stared through the half-open door. A dainty leather purse with ornate golden clasps hung from her wrist. Rita Peterson's blond-rinsed hair was arranged in a proper bun, and she was frowning. Before Marin got to the bottom of the stairs, Rita said, "Hurry up, slow poke! You're at least ten minutes behind schedule as it is."

"What? No, I'm not. You said 3:30. It's 3:30." Marin stood waiting at the foot of the stairs as Rita stepped out, pulled the front door closed, locked the deadbolt, and let the screen slap shut.

Rita hurried down the stairs. "I don't like coming in late and having to sit in the front at these foolish senior functions. It's embarrassing."

"You're not going to sit. We'll be walking around. This is a quilt show. An Exhibit of Early American Quilts. I thought you said they sent you a program."

The pudgy blond-haired woman sighed. "They did. I left it somewhere in the house." She turned, calling over her shoulder, "Pick up the pace, Marin. I've got the car idling."

They went around the side of the house to Rita's smoking, dirt-brown car. Marin shifted her bulging black-and-white satchel from her right hand to the left and pushed her wire frame glasses up on her nose. She opened the passenger door and got in the old Impala.

"Where's this show at?" Marin asked.

"Some Martin Luther King Center near the capitol. I've got it written down on that Post-it on the dash." Rita slammed her door so hard it hurt Marin's ears. "I just hate St. Paul. It's bad enough with all these new housing developments cluttering things up here in my little township, and now we have to pick our way through St. Paul. They should have named it after St. Jude, the saint who looks for lost things, or was that St. Anthony?" She paused with a frown on her face. "Oh, well. Doesn't matter. Why couldn't it be organized, like Minneapolis— where the streets run north and south, east and west, and the avenues are laid out orderly-like? St. Paul is just a mess. A complete mess. Whoever planned that city ought to be shot."

"Oh, Mother," Marin sighed. For a moment she imagined herself getting out of the car and trudging back to the bus stop, but she put the thought out of her mind as her mother flipped the gearshift out of neutral and backed out.

"I'm just setting out the truth as I see it, same as you would. Do I complain about your snippiness?"

In a tired voice Marin said, "I'm not being snippy. If you don't like the streets, then I'll drive."

"Forget it. I'm managing perfectly." She steered wide around some tin cans lying in the gutter.

"Then why in the world do you demand I come with you to these things? You don't need me along. You never even let me drive."

"Don't be silly. It's dangerous out there. Somebody has to come with me, especially since your father's passing. You're the one who insists I get to these cultural events. Isn't that what you said—'Attend cultural events, Mom, or you'll go stale'? If you want me to race all over hell and tarnation, then you have to come along every so often. Besides, what else do you have to do alone in that apartment of yours? I still don't understand why you moved out."

"In case you haven't noticed, Mother, I'm twenty-seven-years old now, and I like to have my own space. Plus, you *know* I'm not alone. I've got Beth."

"Oh," Rita said. "Her. I have no idea why you live with such a person. You've always been so foolish. And this business about having your own space isn't worth the money it costs. Your rent is more than my house payment. You can't even afford a car. Think of the expenses you'd save."

Marin rolled her eyes, looked out her window, and tried to stop listening as her mother babbled on. *A broken record*, she thought. She smelled the scent of pine from the evergreen tree deodorizers hanging from the rearview mirror and the glove compartment knob. Under the pine odor, the car smelled sour.

They approached a railroad crossing, and she saw the tiny piercing light of a train rumbling toward them, still a half-mile down the tracks to the right. As they passed over the tracks, crimson lights began blinking, and the crossing arm came down behind the car. Marin was surprised when her mother didn't seem to notice.

Rita zipped off the side street and merged into the traffic heading down the busy boulevard. Marin wondered how her mother could be comfortable driving hunched over the steering wheel and sitting so close.

"Why is this shindig at a civil rights center?" Rita asked.

"That's not a civil rights center. It's a community center. They must have decided to hold the quilt exhibit there to have more room for the displays."

"Hmmm. You know how I've always loved quilts, but I never had the time to sew much. Your father was always taking you kids camping and biking and hiking and fishing. Who had time?"

Marin squinched up her face as if in pain. She couldn't remember her mother ever darning a sock or sewing a button on a shirt, and she definitely couldn't recall any homemade quilts lying around. She was certain her mother had always bought regular blankets and bedspreads from Sears. She thought of the linen closet in her parents' house, upstairs near her old room. It was a cavernous walk-in closet of narrow shelves packed full of sheets and towels, shoeboxes of treasures, galoshes, pillows, and half-empty bottles of perfume. When she closed the closet door behind her, Marin could still see a shaft of light from the hall inching in through the gap between the door and the frame. Everything sounded muffled when she hid there under the low shelf, and no matter how loud her two sisters got or how much her mother screamed, she felt safe.

Marin changed the subject. "You did bring a map this time, didn't you, Mom? Don't forget the Science Museum debacle. Forty minutes late, and a total waste of time."

"Of *course* I brought a map. I *always* have a map. Not much good it'll do, what with the ridiculous layout of the city. But don't worry. I asked Arnie for directions—you know he used to work at the Hoist Company before they turned it into the IRS. He assured me all we have to do is get on the freeway, take the exit, turn near the Mexican restaurant, then up to another street I forget the name of. I've got it all written down."

"Wasn't it Arnie who gave you directions to the Science Museum?"

"What's your point?" Rita asked in a loud voice. "Quit worrying. I've always found my way home. Sometimes it may be just a little circular, but who cares? I read once that the journey is supposed to be the reward. So consider it an adventure."

"Great. An adventure. I sure hope this beater of yours is running better than last year when the alternator went out in the middle of the freeway. Sounds a little tinny to me."

"My chariot is running fine now, thank you. I had it tuned-up by that neighbor boy who is taking a mechanics class at the Vo-Tech. Do you hear the power?" Rita revved the accelerator. "It's got a lot of get-up-and-go for a car fourteen years old."

"Get-up-and-go? Mother, it sounds like a Nazi tank."

"That's enough from you, young lady. I won't have it."

Marin's head was beginning to hurt, sooner than it usually did around her mother. She pressed the tips of her fingers to her temples and rubbed in a circular motion.

"Look on the dashboard, Marin. What's the address there on the Post-it note?"

"I can hardly read it. Looks like 'Iggenhurt.' Never heard of it."

"Arnie said the place is close to the capitol."

"We passed the capitol ages ago."

"What? I never . . . you didn't . . . It doesn't matter now. You were yapping so much we must have missed the exit. I think I'll take . . . Dale Street. Somebody told me it was right off Dale, but I can't remember—is that the place where the slums are?"

"Whoa, whoa! Wait just a minute there, Mother Dear. I thought you said you knew exactly where we're going and that you had explicit directions."

"Oh, I do. I do. Be patient."

They reached the end of the exit ramp, and Rita stopped for the light. "Now, is north left or right?"

Marin felt her face go red. The blood pounding in her ears made a whooshing noise, the same noise she heard on amusement park rides, especially the rollercoaster. "How should I know! You're the one who's supposed to be so directionally literate."

"Okay, let's go left." Rita eased the car through the light and crept along down the street. They passed over the freeway and headed down Dale Street. The day was growing darker, though some of the storm clouds had dispersed. "We're not supposed to get as far as Summit or Grand Avenue. If we do, we've gone too far."

"Hey, Marco Polo, here's Grand. You better turn around. I knew it! You've gone and gotten us lost, just like last time. Why didn't we take the bus? At least I can follow a bus map."

"No, you can't," Rita said, her voice accusing. "You just pester the bus driver 'til he can't hardly stand it anymore, and then he tells you which buses to take and where to transfer. You're not talking me into riding the bus with you, that's for sure. Last time it took two hours to get to a place eighteen minutes away by car."

Marin shook her head and rolled her eyes. "Face it, Mother, you're lost again."

"No," Rita said firmly, "I'm *not* lost. Why, look. Looky over there." She pointed while sporting a sweet smile on her face. "La Cucaracha Restaurant is right there on the corner. That's the Mexican restaurant I was telling you about. I know exactly where I am. If I turn at the light, I think we pass a bunch of mansions. Maybe the governor's house." Rita maneuvered her way past two cars waiting to turn left and lurched off to the right. "All I want to know is who would name an eating establishment after a cockroach? You wouldn't catch me eating in that kind of place. Bet the governor wouldn't be caught dead in there."

They came to a stoplight, and Marin looked out at the spacious and beautiful apartments and houses in the residential area. She took off her glasses and was rubbing her eyes when her mother said, "Quick! What street is this?"

Marin stuck the lens of her glasses up to her right eye and squinted. "Oxford. We're probably in England now." She jerked forward as Rita slammed on the brakes and careened to the right and around the corner. The car slowed as Rita peered upwards through the front windshield.

"Do you have *any* idea at all where we are, Mother?"

"Not exactly, but if I can catch sight of the capitol, I know I'll find my way."

Marin looked out her window. Vehicles on both sides of the street took up every inch of curb space. Along one curb, she saw a gray car up on blocks. Rusted red circlets covered the body, and all the tires were missing. Wedged between two weather-beaten pickups, the wrecked car looked flat and battered.

"Hmmm," Rita said. "Which way do you think now?"

Marin shrugged her shoulders and remained silent. She crossed her arms over her chest and forced herself to count to ten. Then she began to count the parked cars they passed as her mother twisted and turned through the narrow streets. Marin saw four identical dilapidated houses sagging toward one another like a drunken barbershop quartet. Next to them sat a huge Victorian home, paint peeling, with front porch stairs sloping off to the side. The steps tilted at such an angle she was sure no one could mount them to reach the front door. In contrast, the next two blocks of homes had been restored, painted, and landscaped. The next street had a burnt-out house on the corner with every window covered by wide ominous bars.

"What a shame," Marin said. "So many of these houses would be beautiful if they weren't all boarded up." She turned to her mother. "Where in the hell are we?"

"Goodness, I don't know. Obviously we're headed straight into the ghetto."

"Mom, there are no ghettos in St. Paul."

"There must be. I was watching Jerry Springer just the other day, and he had a whole gang of young toughs on the show from all over the Midwest. And even worse, on Oprah yesterday she brought on these disgusting homosexuals who were complaining about being beat up for being Negro and for being perverts. Can you believe it? In my day, we didn't talk about things like this. It's—"

"Good God! Don't start this again, or I'm getting out! You are goddamn unbelievable."

"Listen here, little girl! There's no need to curse. I won't have it."

With her hands tightened into fists, Marin said, "You *never* listen to me. You don't even try to listen."

Just then, the car jerked to the side and there was a thunk-thunk-thunk sound. Alarmed, Rita looked over at Marin. "Hush. What's that?"

"What do you think? Either you're driving on the curb or you've got a flat tire. Pull over!"

Rita wrenched the wheel to the right and brought the car to a halt three feet from the curb and fifty feet from a stop sign. Marin looked further up the street and across the intersection to the Suds O' Fun Laundromat, a liquor store, and the boarded-up Christ Omnipotent Church of the Redeemed. A chubby black child on a tiny orange bicycle whizzed by, shot across the street, and passed two black men sitting on a bench inside the bus cubicle. A six-foot-high retaining wall to their left was painted bright yellow and in huge letters proclaimed, *Don't Do Drugs. Crack KILLS.*

Marin opened the car door, got out, and slammed the door as hard as she could. Rita jumped and then sat still behind the wheel. Marin pulled her tweed coat down over her pantsuit and bent to tuck her slacks into her boots. Any hair not clamped down by her earmuffs blew wildly in the wind. She squatted to look at the worn right rear tire.

"Hey, Mom! How are you with a tire iron?"

Rita pushed open her door and wormed her way out, narrowly avoiding a passing car.

"What do you mean? Is it really flat?"

"Couldn't get flatter if you sat on it for a year. Do you have a spare?"

"Of course. It's in the trunk, but *we* aren't changing it. We'll have to call Triple A."

"No, I can do it," Marin said. She snatched the car keys out of her mother's hand, opened the trunk, and slapped the keys back in Rita's hand. She took out the jack and tire iron, popped off the hubcap, fitted the iron over the lug nut, and twisted it to the left. It didn't budge. She stood, brushed her hands off, and stepped up on the end of the tire iron and put all her weight on it. Still, the nut refused to break loose. "I can't get enough torque to break it free. Damn. I wish Beth were here. She can fix anything."

"You may think that Beth person is a mechanical whiz, but I didn't raise you to be a motorcycle mama."

"Please! Don't start with me about Beth again!" Marin jerked the tire iron away and threw it overhand into the trunk where it clattered against the metal interior. She picked up the dirty hubcap and pitched it in, too, then slammed the trunk shut. She drew her foot back to kick the good tire, but thought the better of it. With her luck, it would pop, and then they'd have two flats.

Marin looked up and noticed her mother wasn't paying any attention. Rita glared about, her head swiveling like the bobbing ceramic kitty in the back window of her car. The younger woman surveyed the neighborhood of shabby houses. She looked across the street again at the bus waiting area where broken glass glittered on the ground. The two dark figures were still there. Now one sat on the bench inside the cubicle frame while the other leaned against a telephone booth a few feet away. "I'll call Triple A," Marin said. "Do you have your cell phone?"

Rita pursed her lips and looked away. "I checked in the car. The battery is dead."

Marin rolled her eyes and looked across the street. "I'll go call."

Rita shouted, "Have you lost your senses?" She slammed her purse against the side of her leg. "We're in the slums. The ghetto! We have to get away before dark when all those—those drug lords—and those pimps—and—and the gangs come out. You can't go over there. Look at those crooks!"

Marin shook her head and sighed. "I don't think it's that extreme. Nothing is going to happen in broad daylight."

"It's not going to be light for long. We've got to escape. Soon." A note of desperation crept into Rita's voice. "You know how they are. I saw the beatings on the news, and my new neighbor Miriam told me about a TV show telling how all these thugs prey on the elderly at night." Rita's voice started to crack as it rose higher and louder. "It's too dangerous."

"Mom, just because it's a poorer neighborhood doesn't mean a thing. I don't see any roving bands of muggers. I'll be safe using the phone."

"No! You're not listening. Those Negroes over there look like killers. Look at them. They're up to no good. Probably waiting for a drug pickup."

"I think they're waiting for the bus."

"I'm warning you. We're in danger."

"Don't be silly." Marin let out a big sigh as she started toward the phone booth.

"Oh, no you don't." Rita grabbed Marin by the elbow. "You're not leaving me here to be attacked. Come with me." Marin didn't resist as her mother turned her around and pulled her along. A block behind them, a church steeple poked upwards. Without a word, they trudged up the hill to the church, mounted the steps, and tried the door, a huge caramel-colored monstrosity with bands of metal riveted across it. It was locked. Marin rapped until her knuckles hurt. No one answered. They walked around to a smaller door and rang a bell. Still no answer.

"Guess they've all gone home for the day, Marin. What time is it?"

"After four. We're never going to make it to that exhibit. This is even worse than the Science Museum debacle." There was a long silence before Marin said, "For once you must agree. First time you haven't had some smart retort for me."

Her mother looked away. "Let's go sit in the car for a bit and gather our thoughts."

From the front seat of the old Impala, Marin waited impatiently, all the while keeping an eye on the bus stop. The late afternoon light grew dimmer by the moment. "Seems we've got three choices, Mother. I can go up to one of these houses and ask to use the phone—"

"And probably be laughed off the front porch. No one lets strangers in anymore. I, for one, certainly wouldn't."

"Cross off the good Samaritan plan. Okay, then our second choice is to go over to the laundromat and see if there's a phone in there."

"Look at the place. No cars in the parking lot, and the windows are all cracked. It's abandoned."

"Then I should do the most sensible thing, which is to trot over to use the pay phone by the bus stop."

Her mother's face registered alarm. "What if they have guns or knives?"

"Geez, Mom! I can't believe how you exaggerate! They aren't murderers. They're probably just teenagers."

"I'll bet they're carrying switchblades and Saturday Night Specials—all of them are nowadays. My neighbor Miriam and I heard about it on Rush's radio talk show."

"What do you do all day—listen to neo-Nazi skinhead programs? Ever since Dad died, you've become more close-minded and paranoid than ever. This is Saint Paul, for God's sake, not L.A!" Marin smacked the dashboard for emphasis, and the Post-it note with the directions on it fluttered to the floor.

"Ever since you moved in with that Beth person, you've become rude and cranky."

"*Stop* bringing up Beth. This has nothing to do with her. Nothing!"

"I'm just saying that you've become shrill about her and all this freedom and equality business. In my day, women were happy to find a nice man to love and live with. Why can't you be like Susie? Now there's a happy gal. She and your brother and the kids have a great life."

"Oh, please. Give me a break on all that marital bliss crap. I'm not getting married. Ever! Got it? Get used to it. My life is fine as it is."

Rita pursed her lips and crossed her arms. "I doubt it. Look how upset it makes you. I'm not going to stop bringing this up. I carried you for nine months next to my heart. I brought you into the world, held you, fed you, cleaned up after you, and I have a right to guide and protect you until you see the light."

"That's it." She scooped up her bag and opened the door. The world's dimmest overhead light clicked on, casting spooky shadows into the front seat. "I'll be damned if I'll be trapped in here with you one second longer."

She got one leg out onto the pavement before Rita hissed, "Just what the hell do you think you're doing?" She grabbed Marin's coat sleeve in a tight grip.

"I'm *outta* here. I've had it."

"Where are you going?" They glared at one another until Rita abruptly let go of Marin's coat and patted her on the forearm. "Now, now. Let's not be hasty. We should wait here. Someone will happen by soon and see the tire is flat. Or maybe a police car will pass. We have to wait for someone safe."

"Safe? Be realistic. You think it's a good idea to wait in the car until somebody safe comes by? That would probably be tomorrow morning, when we're both frozen to death."

Rita grabbed her daughter's coat again. "We can huddle for warmth—really, we'll be fine."

Marin wrenched her sleeve free and got out. "Are you totally cracked, or what? Why do I even listen to you? I'm going over to use the phone."

Rita leaned across the seat and peered up at Marin. "No! I absolutely positively forbid it. Your father and Arnie both told me you should always stay with your car."

"Since when does Arnie know anything? He's the reason we're lost in the first place. I'm going for help." She stepped back and slammed the car door.

Marin glanced back and saw her mother's frightened face as she sat behind the wheel, shaking her head from side to side and gesturing with both hands through the window. Marin turned away, gripping her bag, and plunged her right hand into her coat pocket. She marched resolutely to the corner, head held high. She looked both ways and crossed the street.

As she stepped up to the curb on the other side, the two men stopped talking and turned to watch her. One was tall and lanky with the sides and back of his head shaved. She could see a round circle of hair, about the size of a small doily, cut short on top of his head. He shifted from foot to foot, shoulders hunched as he pulled at his collar to keep it turned up against the cold. The other man sat shivering in the cubicle with his arms crossed. His hair was shaped so that the top of his head was square.

With every step she took, they appeared younger. *Why, they really are only young teenage boys*, Marin thought as she approached. Both boys wore jeans, high-top sneakers, and lightweight jackets. She could see them shiver as she drew nearer.

Her heart was pounding, and she bumped her satchel against her knee, feeling the heavy weight of her books and purse. She cursed her mother for scaring her. Of the tall one leaning against the metal frame of the phone booth she asked, "Excuse me, but may I use the phone?"

The boys glanced at one another and smiled. "No can do. No way you usin' this phone." Mr. Lanky gestured with his thumb, and Marin saw there was no receiver attached. The coiled metal hung there, the end snipped off.

"Oh." She paused. "Is there a phone in the laundromat?"

"Don't believe so," the seated boy said. "Nearest phone's half a mile or so up at the restaurant. Don't you have a cell phone?"

"No. The batteries are dead."

"Do you need some help over there?" Mr. Lanky asked.

Marin debated for an instant. If she said yes, they'd know she was helpless and stranded. If she said no, they'd know she was lying. So she nodded and said, "I can't get the flat tire off, so I need to call someone to fix it."

Mr. Lanky straightened up from his slouch and looked her over. "We can probably fix it. For a small price. How about ten bucks?"

"Okay," she said. "I think I can scrounge up ten dollars."

"Fine. You got a spare, right?" When she nodded, he motioned to his friend. "Come on, Mike."

Marin and the two boys walked abreast toward the corner and picked their way through the slushy puddles in the street. They reached the Impala, and Marin tried the passenger door.

"Open up, Mother." She pushed the button on the handle but it didn't budge. "Mom! Give me your keys so I can unlock the trunk."

Rita didn't move. She was hunched over, neck and chin retracted into the collar of her quilted coat.

"Mother," she shouted. "Roll down the window and give me the keys." Marin pushed her face close to the window on the passenger side and rapped on the brown door. Her mother sat motionless with a stricken look on her face, so Marin pulled at the door handle again, causing the car to move slightly. She could see the silver keys dangling from her mother's pudgy hand, could almost hear them jingle. Then she watched in amazement as Rita's hand darted forward, inserted the key, and started up the Impala with a *vrrooom*. Rita put the car into drive and jerked forward into Selby Avenue on three tires, the flat thumping.

"Dammit, Mother! What are you doing? Wait a minute. Wait for me!"

The Impala reached the stop sign and turned right as Marin and the two boys surrounded the car, waving, everyone shouting at once. Marin started to run after the vehicle, but the car picked up speed and clunked off down the street. She hurried to step back to the curb to avoid an oncoming car, and then watched the awkward Impala disappear into dimness.

Marin's face burned hot. She dropped her bag against her ankle and turned to face the two boys. Mr. Lanky and Mike shrugged their shoulders, looked at Marin, then gazed down or looked away. Marin knotted her hands into fists.

"Huh," Mr. Lanky said, a puzzled look on his face. "Weird."

"No kidding." Mike shook his head slowly from side to side. "Is she nuts or what, lady?"

The taller boy elbowed him, and in a stage whisper said, "Shut up. It's her mother, you know."

Marin stood with her mouth slightly open. The two of them looked at her as if awaiting an explanation. She resisted the urge to cry and instead kicked a dented Pepsi can five yards down the street, then looked toward the heavens in a silent plea for divine intervention, but saw only threatening clouds. She heard an engine revving and a funny wumping sound before she saw the car. Then the Impala was wobbling down the street again.

"Run! Run!" Rita screamed out a two-inch crack in her window. "I'll pick you up on the next spin down the block." Her words trailed off as the car bumped past. She rolled right on by the stop sign, and the tires screeched as the car, without slowing, again turned right onto the avenue. Marin and the two boys stared after her, mouths agape.

"Totally strange," Mr. Lanky said. "She *must* be crazy." Mike mumbled something at Marin and both boys edged away. She watched them slouch their way across the street back to the bus stop, and her eyes glazed over with tears. Pulling her tweed collar up against the wind, she pushed her hands deep into her coat pockets and stood, her mind spinning like a Ferris wheel.

Down the street, a silver and white city bus moved toward the bus stop and the waiting boys.

"Hold on," she shouted. Mike half turned toward her and waved as she picked up her bag and hurried across the street. Behind her she heard the thumping sound again, and she turned to see the Impala nearing the stop sign. She shook her fist at her mother. Then the bus driver whisked the door open, and Marin climbed up behind the two boys.

The bus was so full she had to stand sideways in the aisle and hang on to the metal bar overhead. The boys stood near Marin and looked at her, both of them frowning. The bus began to jerk forward.

"Hey, lady," Mike said. "Really, you know, you can't leave her out there."

"Yes, I can," Marin said with more force than she expected.

"But it's your ma." He sounded like a very reasonable old man, at least fifty years older than he really was.

A tiny black lady in a thick camel-colored coat reached up and touched Marin's arm. "Ma'am," she said. "It's dangerous out there. If that's your mother, you better do as this young man says. It isn't safe at all out there once it gets a little darker."

All around her the black and brown faces nodded in agreement. She looked around at the concerned faces.

"I wouldn't leave anyone out there that I cared about," said a tall man in a suit, tie, and unhooked galoshes.

"She could get shot," Mr. Lanky said.

"Uh huh, that's right," muttered a chorus of voices.

"They could hurt her."

"Rob her."

"Steal her money, strip her car."

"Yes, ma'am, it ain't safe."

The bus slowed at the next corner as the two boys stared at Marin, nodding.

"Do I stop here or what?" the bus driver asked.

Marin wanted to shout, "No!" but her fellow riders were all clucking and nodding their heads as they ushered her toward the exit.

"Go on now," the tiny black lady said. "Take care of her."

The door opened, and Marin found herself propelled down the stairs and out onto the parking strip.

She stepped back and as she tried to catch her breath, turned to watch the bus roll forward in a slow, jerky motion. The streetlights clicked on, shining into the bus windows, and she watched the passengers peer out at her as the bus moved off. Their faces were bathed in silver light, which illuminated their brown and black and tan faces to a lustrous shine.

Marin heard the old Impala chugging and the sound of metal grating on cement. She felt the cold wind parch her face as she stood, waiting, imagining herself standing in the road forever, smelling exhaust and tasting tears, as her mother whirled past all the rest of the days of her life.

My Lifesaving Journal

Heroic. That's what I've always wanted to be. Someone brave, praised for my courage and altruism. I want to be a hero, like on the TV show *Rescue 911*. Maybe a helicopter pilot, the President's bodyguard, or a paramedic. Somebody important, anyway. Someone people would sit up and take notice of—and respect. Certainly not someone who other children used to call "Little Orphan Fat Girl" in their sing-song, whiny voices.

No—I want to be nothing short of a genuine hero, as daring and valiant as Xena, the Warrior Princess. No doubt about it. That is what I want to be.

I know what it's like to be on the other side of the action because I've been saved. When I was six and we lived in a downtown high rise, my grandmother sent me down the street to the drugstore to buy her a pack of cigarettes. (This was back in the days when the shopkeepers knew all their customers, and with a note from Grandma Alice, I could buy her anything.) I walked toward the storefront, lugging several of my dolls in a flowered cloth bag.

The only thing distinguishing Flynn's Pharmacy from the shops on either side was the white, three-dimensional mortar and pestle floating above the awning in front. A neon red *Rx* blinked in the middle of the white mortar cup as the whole thing slowly rotated. 'Round and 'round it went, and in the late afternoon dusk, I was mesmerized by it. I walked as though half-awake, watching it spinning slowly. Halfway across the crosswalk on St. Peter Street, a screeching sound penetrated my daze. Something struck me from behind and knocked me all the way over to the curb where I landed on my knees. A sweating, bald man in a brown suit landed on top of me.

"Hey!" I shouted, as my eyes filled with tears.

The man panted and kept shaking his head. "Close," he wheezed. "That was too damn close." His face was gray, making him seem haggard and much older than he probably was.

I looked behind me to see a big black truck over the crosswalk and halfway into the intersection. On the side of the truck was a picture of a smiling black and white dog with his tongue hanging out. When the driver's door opened, the dog's tongue bent to the side. A man in a blue uniform got out and stumbled over. He ran his hands through his greasy hair and kept saying, "God, I didn't see her. I'm sorry, I just didn't see her."

By then, a small crowd had gathered, and a nice lady in a lace-trimmed coat helped me up and daubed at my bleeding knees with a lacy handkerchief. I smelled roses, but when I looked around, all I could see was the Flynn Pharmacy in front of me and Rosie's Cafe across the street. There were no trees or flowers. The lace lady pulled me closer to her, and I realized it was she who smelled like wild roses.

The man in the brown suit leaned down and brushed off his pants. Two other men reached out to shake his hand and pat him on the back, and there was an awful lot of congratulating all around. Someone picked up my flowered bag and pushed one of the protruding dolly heads back in. A dozen soft hands reached toward me, steadied me on my feet, and made soothing noises.

"There, there, little girl," the lace lady said. I felt the tears stinging in my eyes. She said, "You must be very careful from now on. Look both ways, dear. You are so very lucky the truck didn't hit you."

As I stood in the gutter, shaken, with torn knees bleeding through my light blue pants, I realized the man who pushed me down had saved my life. Before I could find out his name, the crowd swept him along toward the café, and he disappeared from my sight. The lace lady and another elderly woman in a maroon pillbox hat led me into the drugstore and got bandages for my knees from Mr. Flynn. Then they took me out to a car and dropped me off at the high rise.

I had to turn around and go right back to the drugstore because I had forgotten the cigarettes.

Later in the day, a newspaper reporter knocked on the door. He wrote a story and put it in our neighborhood paper. The bald man, named Cameron Caldwell, was new in town. He had been recently released from prison for kiting checks, and he needed a job.

"She could have been my little girl," he was quoted as saying. "I didn't want to see her get hurt."

His generous action was rewarded by Mr. Flynn, who gave him a job at the drugstore behind the soda fountain counter.

Until I was in high school, Mr. Caldwell worked at the ice cream counter, and whenever I went in for milkshakes or candy or pantyhose or cigarettes for Grandma, he waved and smiled. "There she is! The Little Lady of the Crosswalk. You staying out of harm's way?"

I was always a little embarrassed, but he seemed so pleased, as if he considered himself my personal savior. I connected him with my mysterious father. After my parents were killed in a train wreck when I was three, Daddy must have sent Mr. Caldwell to watch over me and be my guardian angel. It had just taken him a while to find me. And secretly, I felt that Mr. Caldwell was my protector, an ace in the hole to whom I could always turn in case of emergency.

But Mr. Caldwell died of a heart attack when I was a senior in high school, three days after my grandmother died of hers, leaving me totally and utterly alone. To this day, I don't know which of them I miss more.

So I do know what it is like to be saved and to see someone rewarded for his selflessness. Mr. Caldwell was ever after slightly famous in our community. He was often called "The Man Who Saved That Little Girl Back in the 60s," a title which made him so happy, as though he belonged for the first time in his fifty-some-odd years of life.

Being saved was definitely not as fulfilling as being the hero. Most people never even remembered who it was he rescued.

My first opportunity for fame came at the beginning of this summer, and after that, I decided to keep a journal on the topic. I was at Don Dion's Italian Restaurant eating linguine in clam sauce and reading *The Wall Street Journal.* I'm not fond of this newspaper—it's just a bunch of corporate raiders exulting over their piracies. It didn't go well with the hokey background music of Billy Ray Cyrus singing "Achy Breaky Heart" either, but it was the only reading material on the bar. Since I was eating alone, I took it.

It was a slow night at Don Dion's with only one family in a wide booth about twenty feet away from my small table. I saw two frazzled parents, a good-sized baby in a highchair, and two wriggling preschoolers who played with their food and with little toy trucks and cars. The boy, who looked to be about four, stood up on his seat and ran a truck across the top of the booth. The baby kept busy piling up a hill of noodles and red goo on either side of the highchair, while the parents ate, and, in between bites, attempted to keep the baby's squirming siblings from falling into the mess on the floor.

I turned back to an article on employee motivation written by a corporate raider and wasn't paying attention until, out of the corner of my eye, I saw the baby's high chair tipping over backwards. The mother leapt up and grabbed at the high chair, but it was the father who managed to right it before it went over. Instead of a squall, as I expected, the baby was silent.

"Oh, my God!" the mother said. "She's not breathing. Call nine-one-one!" She unhooked the safety belt, wrenched the child from the seat, and stood holding the baby, jouncing her up and down and patting her back. The father sprinted past my table toward the phone around the corner past the bar.

"Hurry, Chuck! She's turning blue!" the mother shrieked.

I don't know what I thought I was doing, but I stood up, knocked my own chair over, and rushed to the woman's side.

"Here, let me see." I reached for the baby, but the mother wouldn't let loose of her child. "I think she's choking, you idiot," I said. "Give her to me!" I snatched the baby out of her arms, put her over my arm, and smacked sharply on her back. The child was heavy, so much so that I squatted down, laid her over my thigh, and gave her several more blows. A round plastic tire the size of a quarter burst out of her mouth and plopped onto my white shoe. I handed the woman the baby, who was by now screaming, her little face all squinched up and hands beating in the air.

Shaking her head, the mother looked around and yelled, "How the hell did that get in her mouth?"

I looked over at the other two children, angelic and quiet in the booth as they stared wide-eyed in fear. "Look no further," I said.

The waiter, the cook, the cashier, and the husband rushed up just then. The woman said, "No biggie, Chuck. It was just a piece of Marky's toy truck."

"Oh great," Chuck said, standing with his hands on his hips and an expression of exasperation on his face. "I suppose I'll have to pay for the ambulance. Shit!"

They turned away to separate the two children who were now punching at one another. As I moved away, I heard the husband say in exasperated voice, "Who's the chubbo? You know her?"

"No," the woman said. "She's nobody."

I walked to my table, righted the chair, and put on my coat. I decided that people are the strangest creatures on earth: totally ungrateful and sometimes downright mean.

I went to the cashier's counter where Pete—that's what his nametag said—waited. His hands were grimy, and he fidgeted with a button on his shirt. He was a young man, probably not even out of high school. With his glossy black hair slicked back, he looked like Al Pacino in *The Godfather*. I realized the waiter and the cook had the same exact hairdo. Maybe it was a requirement in Don Dion's restaurant.

"Wow, Pete," I said, "did you see that?"

"Yeah. Good job. I don't know nothin' about kids. You probably saved her life."

"Could well be. And isn't it nice they wanted to pick up my tab? That guy, Chuck, said to tell you to just add it to his ticket. Said it was the least he could do."

"Sure enough. Thanks a lot, and come again, ma'am." Pete ran his fingers through his hair. As I left the restaurant, I hoped that his greasy hands never touched any of the food.

I went home and watched taped re-runs of *Xena: Warrior Princess*, admiring how she could swoop down from a tree and save someone in the forest who didn't even know she was in trouble. While I ate Chocolate Maraschino Cherry Crunch ice cream, I tried not to think about all the reasons why I didn't belong in this world.

For all the times I dreamed of getting the chance to save a life, I was disappointed by the choking baby. It wasn't the big deal I thought it would be. I decided true heroism requires an audience: spectators who can attest to the bravery. The choking incident couldn't be as fulfilling as, say, running into a burning house and dragging two small children and the dog out into the yard. Then I'd fall coughing onto the grass, while handsome firefighters applauded and news photographers took pictures. What satisfaction that would be. Such glee and excitement!

After the bit in the restaurant, I had daydreams of saving a man by administering CPR, though the prospect of breathing life into the drooling mouth of some stranger did make me feel a little queasy. I watched the video *In The Line of Fire*, starring Clint Eastwood, and imagined myself knocking out a would-be assassin before he could squeeze off a round at the governor. Hey, I'm big enough! If Clint could do it, I'm sure I could, too.

In one fantasy, I caught a baby thrown out of a twenty-story building. That really happened. I read about it in the newspaper a while back. Some guy was walking down the street, glanced up, and boom!

He opened his arms and caught a baby. Did they make him give the infant back? Seems like whoever was so careless should have forfeited their right to the kid.

When I was in high school I took First Aid, and I know how to apply a tourniquet and build splints from pencils, rulers, and sticks. I also took Water Safety in junior high, and believe me, I float. "Big as a boat, look how she floats." That's what the other seventh graders chanted at me. You'd think they thought I had no feelings. But I do float and could tread water longer than any of the cruel, smart-mouth jerks in class. If anyone could pull a drowning woman to safety during a raging flash flood or dive into a swimming pool and save an errant toddler, it would be me.

How many lifesaving chances does a woman get in one life? I was sorely disappointed because I thought my chances were over. Six months passed, and then last week at the child support office where I work as a clerk, I was on break, standing inside the glassed-in reception area out front while eating a chocolate cream puff. I gazed dreamily out the sixth floor window. From there I could see the white mortar and pestle rotating above the awning of Flynn's Pharmacy. I no longer lived downtown, but from the receptionist's window, I was close enough to see the drugstore which, over the years, had been changed and remodeled. But the mortar and pestle continued to turn, and the neon red *Rx* sign still blinked. The mortar was definitely worse for wear, and a dirty pigeon perched next to the pestle where it poked out of the white cup. It occurred to me that I had never in my life seen a pharmacist use a mortar and pestle. I wondered why they hadn't taken down the dilapidated thing years ago.

Just then, a huge man the size of Lurch from the *Addam's Family* came into the waiting room. His eyes and nose were red, like he'd been crying. Or drinking. Or both. He wore a lightweight pea-green coat, with a brown and yellow flannel shirt underneath. He walked up to the counter, bent down, and stuck his face into the hole in the reception window's glass. He told Kari, the receptionist, his wife's name and said he needed her address. Kari was filing her nails under the desk—probably honing them to a point.

"Sorry, sir," she said in a bored voice. "Even if we do have it, we can't give that information out, on account of data privacy." She never looked at him, just kept filing her nails.

"But it's my kids," he whined. "They're my kids, and I ain't seen 'em since before Easter."

He was pleading, and I felt for him. Here it was nearly Thanksgiving, and he just wanted to see his children.

"I'm really sorry," Kari said. She set her nail file on the counter and pushed a piece of paper and a pencil through the slot under the window. "Leave a note, and I'll have someone mail it to her for you. Put down your address and phone number so she can contact you."

"Are you insane?" he yelled. "She won't call me. She don't want me to see my own goddamn kids. She went and got some new boyfriend, thinks he's better than me. I got news for you, though, big news." He reached inside his pea-green coat. Next thing I knew, there was a shiny black gun pointed at her through the round hole in the glass. "Give me the address," he snarled, "or I'll blow your goddamn head off."

I kept my eyes on the man so I didn't see Kari's face, but I thought she was behaving oddly. She just sat there.

"Get it! *Now!*" he roared. He banged the gun barrel between the top and bottom of the hole in the glass, and it made a loud clinkety-clink sound.

"Sure, sure," she said. She grabbed up her nail file and swiveled in the chair. I stood behind her, looking startled, I'm sure.

Wide-eyed, she said, "Wendy, help me! How do I get the address for this guy?" Before I could speak, she launched up out of the chair and pushed past me, banging into my elbow on the way out of the area. She got glaze and chocolate from the cream puff on my chin as she took off down the hall.

I turned back to the man, and he looked as surprised as me. So, here we were, him with a gun and me armed with a chocolate cream puff. "Want some?" I offered him the remaining half of the puff.

"Hell, no," he howled. "I want the address, and I goddamn want it *now*!" He panted as he leaned onto the counter, out of breath, but he kept the gun pointed at me. I set down the cream puff as my body grew colder by the second and my legs shook. I didn't have a lot of time to think, so I just sank down in Kari's chair and said whatever came to mind. "This is for your kids, right?"

He nodded.

"How many you got, sir?"

"There's three."

"Same as me," I said. "Mine are—uh—six, seven, and eight. How 'bout yours?"

"Guess they're two, three and five. No, the boy just had a birthday. They're two, four and five."

"You missed your son's birthday?" I said, trying to ask gently.

"Yeah." He got all choked up, and I could see him fighting back tears.

"This must be pretty hard for you."

"Goddamn right it's hard! It's unfair. The court don't hesitate to take my child support and leave me next to nothing to live on, but when it comes to seeing my own kids which I'm supporting and providing for, nobody will help me. Nobody!" He beat the butt of the weapon on the counter twice, and then lifted his gun arm to wipe his face with his sleeve. "This time, nobody better give me the runaround. That girl better bring back the address, or you're dead."

I looked over my shoulder towards the hall. It was empty, and I knew Kari wasn't coming back.

"Mister, do you really have bullets in that gun?"

"Yep. And I'll use 'em."

"But think about it. I got two kids—"

He frowned as he narrowed his eyes. "Thought you said three."

"Oh, yeah," I hurried to say. "One's with his dad. I have custody of the two girls, and I tell you, I don't get to see my son that often either. It's real rough."

He pressed his face into the glass aperture. "You do get to see him, though, right?" When I nodded, he said, "I don't get to see my kids at all."

"What I'm getting at here, sir, is that if you use that gun and hurt someone, then your kids'll never get to see you. Don't you think they miss you? Don't you think they cry at night about not getting to see their daddy? I know my boy cries for his mom—at least that's what he tells me."

The man was now weeping, which was lucky, because then he didn't see the two policemen tiptoeing through the lobby. He was totally surprised when one grabbed his arm and wrenched the gun out of his hand, while the other got him around the knees and pushed him to the floor. Before I could get out of my chair, they had handcuffs on him and were dragging him to his feet.

"Hey!" he shouted as they pulled him toward the door. "I wouldn't have hurt nobody. Stop! There ain't even any bullets in the gun . . ."

The man and the two officers disappeared out the door, and two other cops came in to take our statements.

I was glad to know I wasn't really in danger all that time, but I also felt cheated. All that stress, all that adrenaline and his gun wasn't even loaded?

I was on the news briefly the same night, too, as was that pushy Kari, who got three times more air time than me. Of course she is small and cute, with fluffy blond hair and nice nails. Flirting with the camera man sure worked for her. Made me real mad. Here she'd gone and deserted me, left me completely at the mercy of what could have been a madman, and then when Channel 3 shows up, she's schmoozing and mugging for the news. I didn't want her to take all the credit, but I didn't want to have to push her aside to get what was rightfully mine either.

Then again, I felt so damn sorry for the man who had lost his kids. He truly was desperate, and it didn't seem right to get any glory from his misery. I didn't blame him for not telling the truth. He wasn't the only one lying. I don't have three kids. In fact, I not only don't have kids, I don't even have a husband. Or a friend. Or actually, any family at all.

Some people say third time's a charm, but I must disagree. I wish I could have stopped at two. Two was more than enough.

See, yesterday, only a week after the incident in the child support office, I was on a break, walking in front of Flynn's Pharmacy on St. Peter Street while eating a hot pretzel with mustard. It was well below freezing, and I could see my breath. My pretzel cooled fast, so I took a big bite. Right then I heard the shriek of brakes locking and tires skidding. I looked across the street in time to see a panel truck run a red light and mash into the side of a dinky Ford Escort.

Before I could swallow the bite, the truck backed up, wormed around the wreckage, and sped off. I chewed furiously and swallowed a lump that felt like a golf ball.

A man in a gray business suit ran by me and into the street, so, with reluctance, I dropped the rest of my pretzel, wiped my hands on my coat, and followed him.

The little Ford looked like half a doughnut. Where there had been a driver's seat, everything was dented in and compressed to the other side of the car. The driver, an Asian woman, sat dazed and scrunched over to the passenger side. The car's engine still ran, making a grinding noise.

"Hey, lady," the guy in the suit asked. "Can you get out?" He reached toward her.

"Don't be grabby," I said sharply. "She might have a back or neck injury." Her face and neck were covered with cuts just beginning to bleed, and there was glass everywhere. The woman held her shoulder at an unnatural angle, too. I couldn't see her body from the waist down. She seemed to be sprouting from the plastic and vinyl of the door, dashboard, and seat. Even though she was a tiny lady, I couldn't figure out how come she wasn't crushed.

Her eyes filled with tears. She pointed toward the back seat with one arm as she cried and spoke in another language. I had no clue what she was saying.

"Can you turn off the engine?" the man said to her. "Lady, turn off the car. Please, ma'am." To me he said in an excited voice, "We need to shut it off, just in case of explosion."

Men are so dramatic. I reached in, felt around next to what was left of the bent steering wheel, and turned the key, then pulled the key ring out and tossed it onto the sea of glass spread over the flat spot that used to be the dashboard. Satisfied, the man backed away, and when I looked around, he had disappeared.

I leaned into the gaping hole that had once been a window and took the woman's hand. She grimaced and continued to gesture and—it sounded like—to plead with me. I patted her and kept telling her things would be all right. Though I knew she didn't understand my words, I tried to sound soothing. Her face grew more ashen, and inch by inch, she slumped forward. Her grip loosened, and suddenly a chill washed over me. "It's okay," I said. "Come on, lady. Hold on. Hold on!"

I heard sirens getting closer, and then, in the dim afternoon light, finally saw flashing red and yellow lights. Car doors slammed, the ring of people around the car parted, and emergency techs pushed through carrying red and white medic bags.

I stepped back to get out of the way and stumbled against the curb. A hand braced me up from behind, and I heard a deep voice say, "Steady there, ma'am." When I glanced back, I wasn't sure which of the many businessmen standing in the huddle had spoken.

A fire engine succeeded in winding its way through traffic on the one-way street, and a whole team of fire fighters leapt from the cab and from the sides where they'd been clinging like barnacles on a ship.

"Jaws of life!" one fireman shouted to another. Police cars blocked off the intersection and were now re-routing traffic. An officer hollered, "Who's a witness? Step forward."

A hand pushed at me from behind. I looked over my shoulder at a young woman who said, "That cop needs your statement."

I pulled my tan coat tighter and realized the whole right sleeve was smeared with blood. I approached the cop, and hard as I tried not to cry, tears leaked out, even though I pushed them back. I told the officer about the panel truck leaving the scene of the accident. I even remembered the first three letters of the license plate, which the cop wrote down in a hurry. I had to shout to be heard over the growling of the machine that was pulling apart the car in order to free the woman. The noise stopped abruptly, and I watched as the firemen extricated the woman from the wreckage and placed her on the ground. Four paramedics, two on either side, knelt over her as though praying. Two of them began CPR, while the other two fiddled with cords and needles, straps and tubes. They worked on her for the longest time. When they gently strapped her on a stretcher, I just knew she was dead.

Suddenly there was a flurry of movement by the Escort. "Whoa up!" a fireman shouted. Three others came to his side and helped him pull away the jagged pieces of metal. The top half of his torso disappeared as he burrowed into the car. He emerged with a toddler cradled in his arms.

Paramedics rushed over with a gurney for the child as a crowd of firemen crouched around.

"Ma'am?" The officer cleared his throat. "Excuse me—ma'am? Can you describe who was driving the hit and run vehicle?"

I was trying to see around the mob of bystanders. "No, sir," I said, hardly able to breathe. "I didn't see any more than I've told you. Excuse me."

Shaking and weeping, I pressed my way through the gawkers and peered around an fireman's shoulder at the paramedics working on the tiny figure. The little girl's eyes were open, but she looked straight ahead, blankly, as though she were in a trance. Then her legs kicked, and I heard a whimper that escalated into an all-out scream. It sounded like she was wailing, "A-maaaa. A-maaaa . . ." In any language, you could recognize the cry: "Mama. I want my Mama."

They had to strap her down to keep those little piston legs still. After putting a blanket over the tiny body, they rolled her, still sobbing, toward the square red and white paramedic van.

"Goodbye, little girl," I whispered. "Goodbye."

A policeman blew a whistle and shouted, "All right, folks. Everybody out of the street. Let's get the traffic moving again."

I stumbled back and would have tripped over the curb again had it not been for a man grabbing my sleeve. I shivered and pulled my coat tighter across my belly. I couldn't stop crying.

The window of Flynn's Pharmacy reflected the light of the afternoon sun, and the mortar and pestle above turned, making a scratching sound as it went. I leaned against the window and stood shaking, staring at a display of close-out sunglasses. *That should have been me. I have no one and nothing. Why couldn't it have been me?*

Just then I felt a tap on my shoulder. "Lady," someone said. The scent of roses wafted over me, and for a moment I felt six years old again. "Lady?" the voice repeated. I squinted and brought into focus the face of a leather-clad, teenaged girl. Her short black and purple hair stood on end, and each of her ears had about twenty earrings dangling. Bloodshot eyes overrun by eyeliner peered at me. She was covered with keys. I mean, every place a key could be hooked, there was one. Keys hung from her belt, from her zippers, around her neck, even laced into her shoestrings. She made a shimmery, clinking noise when she moved.

"Lady, are you okay?"

"No. I'm not." More tears spilled out, and I wiped my face on my clean coat sleeve. "That woman—I think she died. That little baby's mother is dead."

The girl, she couldn't have been more than sixteen, nodded. "Bummer," she said. "I saw you trying to help, but hey, there wasn't anything you could do."

"It should have been me," I said. "I almost died in this intersection myself once when I was little. Maybe if I had died, maybe—"

"Bullshit," the girl said. She crossed her arms over her leather jacket. "It isn't your fault, lady. Shit happens." She pulled a pack of cigarettes out of a key-encrusted pocket. "Want one?"

"No, thanks."

The girl stood staring at me. I don't know why, but I thought I owed her an explanation. "It may be my fault, kind of. I mean—I started keeping a journal about saving lives, being a hero. And then stuff like this started happening all around me."

"Where do you *live*, lady? Like, for real, this stuff happens all the time. You'd have to be living in a hole not to see it, all the accidents and murders and robberies and rapes. Jesus! You're telling me you just now started to notice?"

She made me uncomfortable. Who was this snot-nosed sixteen-year-old to tell me what's up? "This kind of thing just didn't happen before I started the journal. Nobody died. People weren't so cruel. Now I think I've jinxed myself."

"Well then, shit-can it." She lit her cigarette and took a long drag. "Better yet, finish it off the way you want it all to end, and then throw it out. Just shit-can the whole fuckin' thing—the journal, I mean. Outta sight, outta mind."

I didn't know what to say. I looked at my watch and found it had been over forty minutes since I'd left on my fifteen-minute break, so I turned away.

"Hey, take it easy, lady."

"Yeah, you too," I said to her.

"By the way, you got any spare change?"

I gave her three dollars and went back to the office. My boss started to yell at me, but then he saw my face and all the blood on my coat. He listened to my account and let me go home sick. I didn't go back to work for the rest of the week.

The leathered key girl said to shit-can the journal . . . But I'm not going to. Maybe one of these days I'll take her advice and finish it off the way I want it all to end. But right now, two months have passed, and I still don't have the energy.

But one thing she said does make sense. She said to finish off the lifesaving journal the way I'd like it to end, and I have been thinking about that a lot lately. It seems to me that praise and acclaim from strangers isn't really what I want after all. As far as I can tell, what good does it do to save someone else when I haven't even managed to save myself?

I went back to Flynn's Pharmacy the following Monday, and I bought my last Milky Way bar. It's the last bar for two reasons. First, they're tearing down the building to make way for a new parking ramp, so Flynn's is going out of business after all these years. But second, I'm not going to eat all this crap anymore. It isn't making me happy, and I am tired of being so heavy. I think I can change that. I joined the nearby athletic club, and I'm walking on their walking path for an hour after work every day. Already I have lost two inches around my middle. For the first time this winter, my coat, which the dry cleaner did manage to get the blood out of, fits much better.

I am not going to follow that girl's advice and shit-can this journal. I'll pack it away in a box in my closet, and maybe once in a while, I'll still think about it. But not very often. Instead, after all that has happened, I've decided I'm going to focus on the only life I might be able to save, and that's my own.

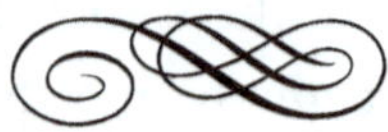

A Letter From Father

November 30th

Dear Rosie,

I got your Thanksgiving card and letter last week and have been mulling over what to write back. Now it's after midnight and very quiet, so it seems like a good time to try to forge a reply. First, let me say your letter filled me with such great pain—but not for the reasons you'll assume.

All these years, all this time, I thought you just didn't like me, that you'd outgrown me, just didn't need me. And here after all these years, it's been a secret keeping us apart, and I didn't have a clue.

So, I felt terrible to read about you and this Marianne person I've never met and wasn't even aware of. Ten years, you say? Was that a 10—your handwriting is still as bad as mine—but I am sure you wrote ten, right?

How can you live with someone for ten years and never mention it? Well, I guess I understand your feelings. You are right. Years ago, I likely did say something about rather having any child of mine "be dead than homo," which was totally insensitive and wrong of me.

Rosie, please understand, people change. I don't think that way anymore. Why, believe it or not, for a few years Minnesota has had a law to protect the rights of gay people all over the state. And I even voted for it! Seemed only fair. You probably heard that Canada is approving laws for same-sex marriages, too. The world is changing all around us. Honey, I didn't know what I was talking about back in the old days. It was fear. Small-mindedness on my part. Everyone so damn picky and afraid of anything unusual or different.

And believe me, Rosie, you were unusual and different! With your three older sisters, I thought I had the corner on the market, the edge on the non-existent instruction manual that should have come with them when they were born. We were blessed with you later in life, when I thought I knew everything about raising daughters. Hell, I'd been through pink bicycles, ice skating lessons, ballet shoes, prom dresses, riding herd over curfews, and listening to your oldest sister's never-ending tales of woe about her latest boyfriend.

Then you came along, feisty and determined, wanting a boys' bike, camping trips, kites, and tree climbing privileges. You wanted to learn how the car worked, and you *LIKED* mowing the lawn. Honestly, I thought you'd grow out of it.

By the time you were the last one left at home, your athletic shoes alone were practically sucking all the discretionary money out of the budget! (That's a joke, honey.)

I know I was hard on you. I was pushy. You were right in your letter—I was controlling and overbearing. Your mother and I just didn't know what to do. Nobody ever mentioned that we could have a child with such a will of her own who refused to conform to the standards of the time.

Oh, but things have loosened up now, and me? I'm so loose I'm falling apart! After your mother died last winter, things haven't been the same. I've done a lot of wondering since the funeral. I couldn't understand why you only stayed until it was over and then flew right back to San Francisco. I found myself thinking back, and I wracked my brain trying to figure out what I'd done wrong to make you run away again, just like you did after you graduated high school.

Since the funeral, I came to realize that we're blessed with people in our lives for only a little time, and then they're gone. I was blessed to have your mother for 51 years, but I was only blessed to have you in my life for 18—and you haven't died! You're still here on earth, and after 16 years, truly, I want you back.

You were also right in your card—that I probably couldn't say these things face-to-face, just like you might not be able to say them in person either. I've never been much good at talking about personal or emotional things. Believe me, after the big war ended in '45, I had a hell of a time simply asking your mother to marry me. She didn't make it easy, didn't speak up or help me. She made me spell it all out and say all the words. You are very much like her and always have been. You both had that stubborn determination, and woe befall the person who crossed you.

Maybe that's why I'm surprised it has taken you so long to confront me with this. Remember when you were 13 and wanted a motorized trail bike like all your sisters' husbands had? You waged a merciless campaign of reason, threats, begging, the cold shoulder, and the evil eye. For God's sake, your mom and I finally had to give in! Our house was nearly a war zone. Besides, you got all three of your sisters and their husbands on your side, so of course we caved in, against our better instincts. I had visions of you splatted into a tree or dead on the side of the road. But you were a careful operator, never one to take dangerous risks.

By the way, Rosie, we've still got that bike in the garage. Every once in a while, your nephew Paul—Lila's kid, he's 14 now, you know—every so often he goes out and gazes longingly at it. I keep telling him we don't have the key, that Aunt Rosie must have taken it with her. Don't be surprised if someday you get a letter in the mail from Paul asking if you still have the key and can he have it.

Anyway, the final issue is about this baby you and Marianne are having. I wasn't clear on who was carrying this child, you or the other gal? Well, somebody is seven months along now, and I hope healthy. No, I don't care if you used scientific means—isn't that what science is for?

I sort of hope it's you having the baby. I like the names you picked out—Jordan and Emma. I can understand why you wouldn't want to saddle him with my moniker—Wilfred hasn't been a fun name—but by all means, if it's a girl, do name her Emma after your mom. Your mother would have been pleased. I think all the other girls thought Emma was an old-fashioned name, though you know little Megan and also Sarah have it for their middle names.

I can't think of what else to tell you except you're wrong about not being welcome here. This house is always open for you—come in the middle of the night for all I care. I'm 71 years old and tiring. Isn't a thing going on here most of the time. Biggest excitement I've had lately is losing a nice, fat walleye up on Mille Lacs and only catching a bunch of teeny ones. Martin (remember Martin Lundquist from the next block?) out-fished me again. But I remind him he has the advantage of being a year younger. And it's his boat, too.

I've always hated writing letters, but for you, Rosie, I'll do it, especially since writing is a far sight better than trying to talk on the phone! Please write me soon and let me know how you and Marianne and Baby Emma/Jordan are doing. And please try to understand and accept my apology . . . please?

Love Always,

Dad

The Jungle Garden

Most ordinary Sunday nights, Helen and Alex locked their doors, turned on the telephone answering machine, and hid from their worries. They rolled the television on its stand into their room and headed for the four-poster bed to watch old video movies like *Casablanca*, *On the Waterfront*, and *Shane*. Snuggling in for the evening, they ate popcorn and blueberry muffins and tried to catch the butter and crumbs before they fell on the patchwork quilt.

On a rainy Sunday in August, very near the end of *The African Queen*, the phone rang and clicked over to the answering machine.

"Helen, your grandmother passed on at the St. Francis Rummage Day Sale earlier today. Thought you'd want to know."

Helen grabbed up the phone. Breathlessly she said, "Mother! I'm here. What happened?" Jerking up into a sitting position, she kicked her legs out from under the quilt.

"Grandma Gertie died today. She had just made a big sale on those crocheted deer figures she makes for rolls of toilet paper on the top of toilet tanks. The friend she set up the table with said she just stopped talking and slipped off the folding chair to the floor like a limp rag. The poor old dear." Her mother's sad voice trailed off.

Helen was having trouble following her mother's narrative. *Poor old dear?* When Helen's father had died twenty years earlier, his mother, Gertie Henderson, took it upon herself to guide and instruct her son's children. She'd have done it, too, except Helen's mother stood in the way. Not a month went by that Gertie and LeeAnn Henderson didn't fight. When Helen heard shouts and shrieks from the living room or kitchen, she ran outside and hid under a huge old bush in the side yard. She clutched onto the thick, heavy stalks of the bush and pulled the leaves around her so no one knew she was in there.

When Helen grew older and the bush no longer served her purposes, she retreated to the room she shared with her older sister, Monica. They turned on the radio and waited silently until they felt the front door slam. Looking out the window from above, Helen would see her Grandma Gertie's swirl of gray hair and watch her stocky body marching out of the house to her car. For the rest of the day, Helen's mother would wear a pleased, smug look.

Her mother interrupted Helen's thoughts, "I've got to hang up, Helen. This is costing me money. I suppose you couldn't make it to the funeral." Her voice trailed off again.

"What? Mother! Of course, I'll come. When is it?"

"Thursday morning at Gertie's church, the House of Hope. The visitation is Wednesday night. Call Monica. I told her she was going to have to pick you up at the airport tomorrow."

"No, Mother. I think I'd rather drive. I could be there by Wednesday afternoon."

"All right. Suit yourself," her mother said, and without a goodbye, she hung up.

Helen sat shaking on the edge of the bed. Out of the corner of her eye she could see Katherine Hepburn and Humphrey Bogart swimming, but then her eyes filled with tears. She clenched her fists and fought back the wave of sorrow that welled up in her.

Alex turned off the video and held Helen until she eventually cried herself to sleep, where she tossed restlessly.

Monday morning she felt drained and frightened. *I know what I have to do, and I can do it.* She rose and set to work. Alex sat in the breakfast nook drinking coffee. Helen kept her eyes downcast and tried to act brave and nonchalant as she packed and rushed around the house. After a while, Alex rose and followed Helen into their bedroom.

"Can I help?"

Helen stuffed two t-shirts into her bag. "I don't think so."

Alex waited. The suitcase was nearly full when she set her mug on the bedside table and took hold of Helen's shoulders, waiting until Helen looked up.

"What's the matter?"

Helen shook her head. "I—I don't know." She sank down to the bed. "I can't—I can't face this, Alex. I'm not going."

"Yes, you are. You *can* do this. Come on. I'll help you load up."

After putting the big gray suitcase in the cargo area of the hatchback, Alex said, "If I didn't have the bar exam Wednesday, I'd be going, too. I'm sorry I can't be there with you. You know you can call me anytime."

"I wish you could be with me, too," Helen said as she began to cry.

They hugged for a very long time. As Helen drove away, she looked back and tried to draw strength from her final glimpse of Alex waving.

Now on the road without Alex's warmth and humor, she felt so alone. She watched the winding road flow by the parched countryside and thought about the difference between Washington and Minnesota. It wasn't just the weather.

Helen's family could not understand how she could have left the West Coast and its mild winters, beautiful scenery, and sea green, sap green, jade green freshness. "Mold green is more like it," Helen always said.

It took a lot of rain to keep it that green. Dismal days were what Helen remembered most, and it rained for two-thirds of the year in Seattle. One of Helen's earliest memories was of rocking in a chair with Grandma Gertie and singing, "Rain, rain, go away. Come again some other day."

And come again it always did. Misty vapors, torrential showers, sleet, and hail. Never a lack of water.

Despite the warm breeze blowing in the car window, Helen shuddered. Going back to all that rain and verdant greenery stifled her. Unlike the cold, clean snow she had come to respect and trust in Minnesota, the thought of the rain and vegetation of Washington made her feel clammy and shaky. Grandma Gertie had lived near Puget Sound all her life, and gray days never bothered her. Gertie always said, "Living in a city where you can smell the sea breeze, see the mountains, and still be near all the best flea markets in the world is where it's at. Anybody'd be crazy to move from this beautiful place."

Gertie never did move from that beautiful place. Until now. Helen felt shocked by her grandmother's death. It didn't seem real. *Grandma will be eighty-nine this August—would have been eighty-nine*, Helen corrected herself. She remembered Gertie had worked until she was seventy-two. She was scheduled to retire at age sixty-eight, but after the big birthday celebration, she kept appearing each morning at the faded little laundry shop, Moon's Laundry and Mending, on Fifth Street. Finally, the proprietor pried the iron right out of her hand and nudged her past the customers into the dusty foyer. Gertie stood at the door, dazed, in her blue heavy-duty work apron.

"Gertie, you retired now! Time for you go home! Be with family. Live own life," Mr. Moon said as he ushered her out the door. "Come back. Visit us. For you, we do laundry free."

For years after, whenever Helen stopped in with her dry cleaning, Mr. Moon told her what a good worker Gertie had been. "It hard to let Mrs. Gertie go. But daughters need job. Sons get married, and suddenly I have more daughters again. What else I do?"

After the job ended, Gertie stayed home. Weeks passed. She didn't seem to know how to occupy herself, and Helen worried about her. Gertie called her sons and daughters daily. She called the grandchildren. She even called her great-grandchildren, though they were only toddlers.

Then she started visiting.

The battered yellow Ford Falcon zipped across town, vinyl top peeling and flapping against the windows. Her pudgy, barrel figure tumbled out from behind and below the steering wheel. With delighted squeals, the children raced to greet Grandma. She always carried special treats: a stray dog in the back seat, a package of day-old fortune cookies, scarves and cans and trowels and odd trinkets. Sometimes she opened the four car doors and said, "Let's clean out the car. Any money you find is yours to keep, and I'll take you down to the candy store."

Helen was shy and held back, but Gertie always made sure she got a dime or a quarter. Then all the kids piled into the car and careened the four blocks to Sally Mae's Candy Corner.

The parents frowned to one another as they tried to steel themselves for her barrage of fast-paced conversation. It was impossible to know when she would go home. Helen watched as the family tried to work around her. Just when it seemed inevitable that Gertie would stay for supper, she bolted up from her chair and headed for the door, patting children's heads and behinds. The grownups sighed with relief.

Gradually, Gertie settled into a new pattern more frenetic than her old work schedule. She sold Tupperware, Shaklee products, Aloe Vera, Amway, and sometimes Mary Kay make-up, though she didn't use it herself. Her living room looked like a stockroom for Direct Sales International. She used her dining room for a workshop to build wooden birdhouses and picture frames. She knitted and crocheted pink and blue blankets and booties and psychedelic toilet tank covers to sell at craft shows.

Gertie didn't make much money, but she managed to give each member of her growing clan a Christmas gift every year. One Christmas, every person from age two to eighty-one received a pair of matching hot pads. Each set was different from every other. Another holiday season, she gave out tins of anesthetic balm wrapped in shiny Reynold's Wrap foil and tied with a red ribbon. She got the balm on a special sale through a feed and farm magazine. Helen never used the salve, but she liked to pop the lid off from time to time to breathe in the fragrant smell. Many years passed, and she still had the old green can. The ointment finally dried up, so Alex punched a slot in the top, and they saved their change in it.

Helen shook herself from her memories and realized she had been driving for several hours. The gas tank was low, and she resolved to fill it as soon as possible. She never liked to drive with less than a quarter tank, something she had learned from her grandmother. When she was ten and Monica eleven, she recalled spending two weeks at Grandma Gertie's. Half the neighborhood children, including Alex, were with them on the way back from a closeout sale at Polly's Potted Plants when the car started thumping and clumping. Gertie wended her way over to the shoulder of the road.

It was a rare sunny day, and Gertie clucked and worried more about the twenty-five or thirty plants on the floor, under the seats, and nestled between the children than she did about their predicament.

Leaving six children and thirty plants frying in the car with doors locked and windows rolled up, Gertie went marching down the highway for help.

Minutes later, a shiny Chevy Bel Air coupe pulled up, and Gertie and a Roman Catholic priest jumped out, gas can in tow. Between Gertie's garrulous explanations, the priest filled the tank, blessed the car and its contents, and made the children promise to attend church and pray every night. Helen didn't have any problem with his request. She'd just spent the last few minutes praying with such intensity that she figured she had done a whole week's worth of devotions. The priest patted Monica, who was hanging out the now-open window, and wished them good luck. He got in his white and blue Bel Air coupe, made a U-turn, and drove off.

To this day, whenever Helen saw a 1950s two-tone Chevy, she remembered that kind priest and how Grandma's crazy competence had come through again.

But she couldn't take any chances on this highway leading through Montana. She had to know she was safe. It was unlikely that a priest would stop and help if she ran out of gas now. At the next exit, she pulled into a service station and filled the tank with super unleaded. She washed the windows all around, wiped the mirrors and headlights, bought a soda and chips, and settled back in the car for the drive ahead.

As a child, and then as an adult, Helen was fascinated by Grandma Gertie. The woman never seemed to stop. Even when Helen's lanky teenage frame towered over her, Gertie kept up a pace Helen envied. Her short, fat legs beat out a staccato rhythm that Helen could hardly keep up with, and her intricate tangles of conversation left Helen spinning.

The older Helen got, the less she could cope with that. She didn't know if Gertie was accelerating or if everyone else's resistance was wearing down.

Gertie didn't want Helen to stay in Minnesota. At least four or five times a year, a hastily written scribble of a letter arrived extolling the excellence of the Pacific Coast or the mountains or the beauty of her budding garden. Without fail, at some point in the letter, Gertie asked Helen when she planned to return "home." Once she wrote, "Haven't you had enough of that fiery, flat land? I was there when I was young, and it was so hot I threw up in a bucket."

Gertie never came out to visit, and Helen felt that if her grandmother couldn't accept or reconcile the distance between them, it was at least partly because of her relationship with Alex. Alex grew up next door to Gertie. When Helen was twelve, Gertie sold her house and moved across town. Over time, Helen forgot her childhood playmate. When she went to college, she was surprised to discover her old friend enrolled there, too. They spent increasing amounts of time together, until their sophomore year when they decided to move into a small apartment off-campus. She and Alex helped one another through school and made plans to move into a bigger place when they graduated and got jobs.

All seemed fine until the Henderson family reunion in July of the year the two graduated. Helen arrived late with the four dozen Kaiser rolls her mother had instructed her to bring. When she laid them on the picnic table, she noticed Grandma Gertie was acting funny. She didn't speak to anyone as she muttered to herself, smacked the baked beans on the table, and raked the coals on the grill.

Helen was puzzled and asked her mother, "What's wrong with Grandma?"

Her mother looked at her, then pursed her lips. She crossed her arms and said, "Well, I wasn't going to mention it, but I think she's pretty upset with you. About that Alexandra." There was an edge of excitement to her voice. "I really didn't mean to say anything to her, dear. I know you told me not to, but she provoked me, and it just slipped out."

Helen stood still for a moment before sitting down hard on the picnic bench.

"Exactly *what* do you mean, Mother?" Helen's voice rose, and she felt her face turn hot.

"I told her you and Alex are—ah—well, more than friends."

Helen stared at her. She felt light-headed. Then she took a deep breath and stood. "I can't believe you. I hate you for doing that. How could you do this to me?"

Her mother stared open-mouthed as Helen turned and fled.

The next day, Grandma Gertie dropped by with a small rubber tree plant for Helen. She didn't say much, and she didn't stay long. But after she left, Helen burst into tears. She and Alex began to talk about moving away from Helen's meddling, interfering family. At first Helen didn't want to go, but as time went on, the friction between her mother and grandmother wore her down. When she was offered a job with a computer software company in Minneapolis, she took it.

Nine years later, the old anger and loss still welled up in a rush. She felt as though her whole life had been a series of losses: first her father in the car accident, then her feeling of belonging, her home, school, and friends, and now Gertie. Tears blurred her vision as she drove down the road, and her throat felt as if it would explode.

I will not cry over this same, rotten stuff, she thought. She turned the radio on. Just static. She flipped the dial around hoping for any station, anything to help her get her mind off the pain, but she was too far from any clear signal. She clicked the dial off and concentrated on driving.

When she arrived in Butte late that night, she stopped at a Hardee's for a sandwich. Scanning the local paper, she found it was full of news about people she didn't know or care about. "Two Die In One Car Accident." "Local Sheriff Accused of Unethical Deals."

The world was a mess.

She went to her room in the motel and went directly to bed. Throughout the night, she had troubling dreams. She dreamt she went to a funeral parlor and found her entire family sitting on folding chairs, staring at the floor, motionless, as if made of stone. She stepped into the room where Gertie was supposed to be, and instead of a coffin, she saw a small cot on which Gertie lay gasping for breath.

Looking back over her shoulder, Helen saw the family waiting, shoulders slumped, faces slack and disinterested. She shouted for someone to come help her, but nobody moved. They sat there in their over-sized dark dresses and pumps, black suits and fat ties, waiting.

Helen rushed to Gertie's side and knelt on the floor by the cot. Gertie was trying to tell her something, but it made no sense. In her small, plump hands, Gertie held a bouquet of red roses. She handed them to Helen. As she opened her hands to take them, they turned into pieces of yellow straw and fell to the floor like so many pick-up sticks. Gertie was dead, and the whole scene floated away, leaving Helen crying and exhausted in a field of yellow grain under an arch of yellow roses.

At seven Wednesday morning, Helen awoke to the persistent shrill ring of the travel alarm clock. She dragged herself out of bed, showered, and tried to prepare herself for the final miles, the arrival in Seattle. All morning she felt tired, and as she drove, bits of last night's dreams drifted in and out of her mind. Recalling fragments of the dream images made Helen cry again. It didn't make sense. Nothing made sense. She tried to stop crying, but couldn't. The more she told herself to calm down, the more she sobbed, so she pulled over to the side of the highway.

She sat there for some time before she recovered enough to decide to drive on to the next exit and find a phone. Seeing the gold and brown Denny's sign up ahead, she took a Missoula exit and wheeled into the parking lot.

Inside the restaurant, Helen was glad to find the public phones in a small alcove adjoining the rest rooms and away from prying eyes. First, she called her own number, but as she expected, Alex was not at home.

She redialed, and when her sister Monica answered the phone, Helen began to cry again. "Looks like I'm not going to make it back to the funeral, Sis."

"Helen? Where in the world are you?"

"Uh—somewhere in Montana. Around Missoula, I think." The receiver crackled a little as Helen shifted and turned away from the restroom entrance.

"Come on," Monica said. "You've come too far now to turn around and drive all the way back home, don't you think?"

"I just can't do it," Helen said. "This is too crazy, too scary. I feel horrible."

"Oh, it won't be so bad," Monica said in the sing-song voice one uses with a temperamental child. "Listen, first off, you're an idiot to stay at Mom's. You really ought to stay with Mike and me and the girls. Personally, I wish I had been the one to call you, but you know how Mother is. She just loves to be the first one to break bad news. They hadn't even wheeled Grandma out of that church bazaar and Mother was already organizing things and calling everyone on Earth. I think she's finally gone off her rocker. She's turned her place into a shrine for Grandma Gertie, too. In fact, I almost think she really misses her. I'm not sure I comprehend it."

"Monica, I can't face this. I should have come out to see her sooner. Why did I wait so long? Maybe this wouldn't be so hard if I'd come to visit—and now I never can." She broke into fresh tears, covering her mouth with one hand while gripping the receiver with the other.

"Oh, Helen! It's not that awful! There are many people out here looking forward to seeing you. I don't understand why you didn't bring Alex with you, though."

"She has the bar exam for the next two days or else she would have come."

"That's too bad. Tell you what—I'll call Mom for you and tell her you're staying with me. She'll grouse about it a bit, but who cares? She's so busy packing up all Grandma's valuables that she probably won't have much time anyway. Please come. We'll go to the funeral together and be moral support for each other, okay?"

"I don't know. I didn't think I would feel this bad. I just can't stop crying, and now I'm so sorry I never came to see her . . . and now it's too late. I guess I really let her down."

"Whaddya mean, *you* let her down?" Monica yelled into the phone. "Are you crazy? You were her absolute favorite. Every time she got a letter from you, she all but read it in church. She was always so proud of you. I can't believe you don't know that. When we were little, she'd always take you, lucky you, out to that jungle garden of hers. I always envied you for that. After I fell down and cut my knee open on the sprinkler head, she wasn't interested in letting me out of the house."

Helen remembered the jungle garden very well. Gertie's two-acre back yard was overrun with weeds and long reedy grasses. Under a gold trellis arch was a cement pond with scummy green water in it. Several tiny goldfish lived there with a huge carp Alex had nicknamed Moby Dick.

Bamboo sticks jutted from the ground around two sides of the pond, and roses and ferns encircled them and wound over onto the trellis. The lot's perimeter was crowded with several towering pine trees interspersed with two crab apples, a walnut, and a plum tree. Helen could still feel the slick pine needles under her feet, and she could see the thick brush and shrubs in her mind's eye.

Between the trees that encircled the lot, Gertie had nailed together wide, flat boards from the ground up to form a fence higher than Helen's head. The fence was meant to keep the dogs and neighbor children out, but there were plenty of ways to crawl over or under and get into the yard. On any pleasant morning, Helen could look up to the second story bedroom window and see Grandma Gertie, with arms akimbo, grinning as a half-dozen small bodies wriggled through the shrubbery or climbed the trees. She didn't seem to mind.

In the middle of the yard was the garden Gertie spaded every spring. She planted flowers and vegetables in a haphazard fashion, and when they came up, they had a tendency to wind together. Tomato plants might be surrounded by marigolds. The overgrown rhubarb leaves covered zucchini squash and cucumber vines. Gertie didn't weed the garden much, yet every year she came up with plenty of vegetables.

Few of Helen's cousins spent any time in the back lot with Gertie. They thought it was creepy and dirty. Helen didn't mind the snakes or bugs or the smell of rotting compost. She liked to dig with Gertie all day.

Sometimes she and Alex made fishing poles with bamboo sticks and pretended to be deep-sea fishermen trying to hook Moby Dick. If it were fall, her favorite time of year, Helen helped pick apples, and she gathered walnuts in a smaller version of Grandma's large burlap sack.

How long has it been since I've planted anything? She'd often teased Alex about her fussing with the houseplants, but how long had it been since she herself had paid attention to growing things?

The year after Helen's father died, Gertie put her house up for sale. Helen's uncles came over with a roto-tiller and scythes. They knocked down the planks and the trellis, poured cement in the fishpond to turn it into a patio, burned the lumber and bamboo, and made the backyard into a respectable looking lot. Helen remembered the confusion and anger she felt when she saw her uncles cover over the garden with lush pieces of sod.

"Nothing lasts forever," Gertie had said to Helen as she packed some seedlings into the trunk of her car. "But, Helen, I'll put in another garden at the new place." Helen didn't understand how Gertie could be so cavalier. She turned away and went to sit on the front porch to wait for her grandmother to take her home.

Helen realized she still missed the wild, cluttered jungle garden, with its overgrown trees and mysterious shrubs. She missed the roomy, yellow house her uncles had painted an ugly, boring shade of gray. Most of all, she ached for Gertie. She longed for the squat, old woman who didn't bother to try to distinguish between flowers or weeds or vegetables, seeing equal value in all of them. But she also realized that Gertie had always loved her, and right now, whether she went to the funeral or not, it didn't matter.

"Helen? Helen? Are you there?" Monica asked. "It isn't like you to call me when you're this upset and then completely ignore what I am saying."

"I'm sorry. What did you say?"

"I asked you what you're going to do? Why don't you scurry over to your car and get your butt out here? This is my first funeral, too, and I wish you'd get here. What's it gonna be? You finishing out the trip or what?"

Letting out a deep breath, Helen said, "Okay. I'll do it." She paused a moment, trying to think what to say. "Thanks for talking to me. I needed that. I'll try to get there before suppertime so we can go to the visitation together."

After she hung up, Helen leaned against the wall, took a deep breath and exhaled, letting her shoulders and neck relax. *I think I'm going to be okay. I think I'll be all right.*

She felt a gnawing in her stomach and realized it had been hours since she had eaten. She stepped out of the alcove and headed to a table. Suddenly, scrambled eggs, toast, and juice sounded wonderful. And maybe a Waldorf salad in memory of Grandma Gertie.

Mouse

I am a mouse, small and timid, cautious and hungry. I creep through the bones of this city searching for shreds of food and human decency, but find little of either.

Day is frightening: the car noise and truck exhaust, people shouting and jostling, the city sanitation workers grumbling, and the deafening roar of their garbage trucks. All of this, plus the panhandlers and thieves and opportunists. I come out in the morning and hide away by noon, then reappear again after dusk.

Night is my refuge, a time when I am a shadow. You might pass me by and never notice my presence, though I see you. I smell your cologne, observe your nervous walk and how you check your watch as though these were to be your last minutes on earth and you had final parting words to make to your loved one.

I am not who I once was. I used to live in a nice split-level home in the Chicago suburbs, complete with a cat and dog and a lover who came home each day from her job as a purchasing clerk for a construction company. By romantic terms, we met late in life—I was a fifty-year-old widow, and she was forty-six. We loved each other very much, but we were mice back then, too. No one could know about our love. Each day I went to my job at an animal grooming outfit and combed out, clipped, and bathed mostly dogs and an occasional cat. And we led our quiet, private life.

We were oh so happy, my lover and me. Eleven years of comfort and happiness, until the day the construction office called and said

Millie had been taken to the hospital after passing out at her desk. It was not a matter of "passing out." She had a serious stroke, followed by a massive hemorrhage, which finished her off inside the week. Swathed in white sheets and bandages on her head, she looked so helpless. They tried to relieve the pressure in her brain, but she died without ever regaining consciousness. Without ever saying goodbye. Without leaving a will. Without realizing I'd be thrown to the tigers, a morsel of defenseless flesh.

Her three brothers, their wives, and an array of teenage children arrived within days. They said not to worry; they would take matters in hand and deal with the estate. They did indeed take charge of Millie's estate, which is to say they made off with everything of value, cleaned out her bank accounts, and began selling things immediately. After initial words of consolation, they forgot me, and each morning seemed surprised to find me still in the house—as though they expected me to evaporate in the night like their beer and soda spills on the coffee table and chiffonier.

The day after the funeral, the oldest brother, Bertram, knocked on the bedroom door and barged in to find me sitting in the Barcalounger chair looking out the window into the backyard. "Ah, hmm, yes. Well, Irene. Have you packed yet?" he asked.

I was shocked. Truly bowled over. I had not gotten used to the idea, the reality, of Millie's death, and now here was her brother inviting me to leave the home we'd shared for over a decade. It was all I could do to say, "What?"

He moved over to the window, his huge, hairy paws crossed over his maroon Izod shirt and his rotund belly folded over gray slacks. "I know this must be hard for you, what with Millie dying and all, but we're going to have to put the place on the market. Paint it up, make repairs, you know. Why, once we take all these geegaws down from the walls, this room alone will need at least one good coat of paint."

I looked around our room at the fine oak chest of drawers and matching bedstead. I took in the beautiful framed ocean and woodland prints Millie and I had bought and hung over the bed the year after I moved in with her. I drank in the sight of sunlight streaming in the windows, shining brightly on the bedside table which held a clock radio, Millie's glasses, and the last book she had been reading, *An Atlas of the Difficult World*, by Adrienne Rich.

"Bertram, this is not what she would have wanted. This is—"

"You got no claim here, Irene," he said, his voice rising. "The others wanted me to pack you up and move you out when we first got here, but I thought it only right to give you a few days. Funeral's over now, and it's time."

When I began to cry, he slunk out of the room in a hurry and pulled the door shut behind him.

I moved through the house as if surrounded by a cushion of thickening fog. In every room was some reminder of Millie. Her hairbrush in the bathroom, still full of her silvering hair. Her favorite cookware spread out on the kitchen counter. A golf umbrella and gardening shoes peeked out of the front hall closet, and there were her shelves of books in the third bedroom, a room now full of sleeping bags and piles of wrinkled and dirty clothes. It got to where I couldn't bear to look around, and soon I was grateful for the fog encircling my head and moving into my mind.

I packed my things: clothes, my favorite pictures, some rain and snow gear, an armload of books, some of our most loved music tapes, and the Indian jewelry we bought on a trip to Arizona a few years back. I gathered up money from the grocery can and took the quarters from the change jar. Other than the money in my purse, I had no funds. Millie did all the finances, paid the bills, balanced the checking account. I hated those responsibilities and was glad to give them up when I moved in.

I called my one and only living relative, my niece Cheryl, in Minneapolis, and told her I had had to quit my job and needed a place to live until I found work. She didn't ask me any questions, and I didn't tell her about Millie, but she agreed to let me stay with her and the kids for a while.

I took the Greyhound, leaving behind all the comfort and security I'd ever known, hoping I could make a home with my niece, maybe help her out with the kids. How was I to know that within days of my arrival, she and her husband would reconcile? He demanded I move on. Her or me, he told Cheryl, and with that kind of ultimatum, who do you think she'd pick—the impoverished and depressed sixty-one-year-old, closeted aunt? Or the handsome, smiling, wage-earning father of her three children?

Cheryl slipped me fifty dollars from her grocery fund and agreed to store some of my luggage in the garage. I gave her my jewelry, books, and pictures for safekeeping.

Meekly—like the mouse I am—I waved goodbye to her and the kids after she dropped me at the downtown bus station. She thought I was returning to Chicago, but there was nothing there for me. Millie was my whole life. With her gone, the place meant nothing.

The first couple of nights, I stayed in a Motel 6. I tried to find work, but it was no use. It was almost laughable. No one wanted to hire an old lady with a sad face whose only marketable skill was dog grooming.

At last, I was forced to go to the welfare people, and though they were nice, they didn't help much. They arranged for me to pick up two hundred dollars per month and food stamps, neither of which is sufficient to afford a place to live. I tried to get one of those places they call an SRO—single residency something-or-other—but the waiting list was six months long. In five months, I'll be sixty-two and eligible for my social security. It won't be much, but still, it'll be enough to get by, and if I get any credit from my dead husband's account, I should be able to make it.

So I have five months to go—actually four months and twenty-four days. I pass the time reading cast-off newspapers, making notes in this tiny journal, and watching the people of the city. I have a new appreciation for the survival skills of the many men and few homeless women I encounter. I never knew there were so many, and you probably don't either because as I said before, we are like mice, scurrying into holes; concealing ourselves behind dumpsters; finding hiding places under stairs, in window wells, or in unoccupied buildings; creeping out only to search for food and warmer clothes.

I have made one acquaintance with whom I hope to become friends. Her name is Marge. It took me over a week to get within twenty feet of her, partly because of the smell, but also because she was afraid of me. I began by catching her eye and nodding, then rising slowly from my seat and taking a food item out of my coat pocket. I'd make sure she saw the Twinkie or half sandwich or bun, and then I'd set it down and back far away. She'd come and snatch it up, then give me a guilty nod and run the other direction. After days of this, she began coming closer, until early one evening she sat down on the other end of the bench in the cool twilight.

Her face was lined and dark with the mixture of sweat, sun, and dirt. She could have been any age, from forty-five to sixty-five; I couldn't tell. I told her my name, and she said, "Marge," then nothing further. I assumed it was her name and have been calling her Marge ever since.

Once I asked her how long she'd been out on the street, and she said "Four winters." I told her she could come to the welfare people with me, but she shook her head and backed away. I tried to explain how she could get a little money to help her, but all she said was, "No ID. No! No ID." I didn't press her.

It is December now, and my social security doesn't come through until early May. Perhaps with Marge's help, I can make it through the long winter. Lately, I find I'm feeling quite mad at Millie. Good God! She was younger than me. I was the one who was supposed to become ill and infirm first, then die—not her. Still, each day I pray to Millie to look out for me. I don't know if she can hear or if she can help, but I keep on. After tomorrow, it's only four months and twenty-three days, and each morning when I awaken, I know I have crawled one day closer to escaping this ugly mousetrap.

   Lori L. Lake

The Big Eddy

*In Honor of the Alsaker Family,
particularly Vina, Kermit and Vince*

Elmer Jorgenson leaned against the corner of the storage shed and watched the girl who stood in his farmyard paying out line from a kite reel. Her cheeks and unmittened hands glowed rosy crimson like her jacket. Elmer smiled. The bow kite began to jerk and dip. "You're in a bad current, Nealy. The wind is too strong up there. Roll her in some or you'll lose her."

Nealy spun the wheel with an awkward force, and in seconds, the kite calmed. "This is good, Mr. J. This way I can see the pattern I drew. Don't it look pretty up there?"

"Indeed." He eyed the swirls of indigo, red, emerald green, and turquoise she had colored on the kite's face. The kite was a welcome contrast to the flat soybean and wheat fields, the drab sky, and the leafless trees around the storage shed and outbuildings.

"When I get good at this," Nealy said, "you're going to let me have a try at that big Eddy kite you and Ben built, aren't you?"

Elmer nodded. "Sure. Or else Ben will, when he's back from overseas."

Nealy's three older brothers had each, in turn, learned to build and fly kites well enough to be trusted with the giant nine-foot kite Elmer and his son had built years ago. The Eddy kite was difficult to launch. It took two people to handle both the main bridle and the secondary bridle near the tail. But once aloft, it was a beautiful sight to see, all silver, red, and black. If Nealy kept practicing, he knew she would be able to fly the big kite one day soon.

"Nealy, you did a good job fastening the plastic to the spars. You've built a sturdy kite." He knew his words pleased her.

She grinned. "Yup."

"Guess I'll get back to work on that pesky leak," he said. "Give me a holler if you need help bringing her in. Oh, and don't forget, your mother said to get home for noon supper."

"Okay, Mr. J." Elmer watched her reel the string in . . . in . . . in, then out a few feet, then in again. He grabbed his bucket of tools and climbed the ladder to the roof of the storage shed. He set the bucket down at the crest of the roof and lowered himself to one knee to insert a tube in a caulking gun, then spread the gooey black tar in the shingle cracks. He was halfway across the roof when Nealy called out, "Somebody's here, Mr. J."

Elmer fumbled to snap the release on the caulking gun. A sleek black car slowed to a stop in front of the white farmhouse. From his kneeling perch on the crinkled roof, Elmer saw two tall shapes in green suits getting out. He let go of the gun and it slid down the roof a few feet before coming to a stop on a wet patch of tar. Scrambling to the roof's edge, he lowered himself a few rungs down the ladder and jumped the remaining five feet to the ground. Nealy's kite string was slack, and she wasn't watching it at all, but Elmer didn't stop to warn her. He wiped his hands on his coveralls as he hurried across the farmyard toward the house. The rarely used front door of his two-story farm house opened, and he saw the pale blue speck of his wife's apron, made out her tousled white hair, saw her hands come up to her face as the two soldiers stood on the porch.

Now he passed the barn and the chicken coop where hens pecked and squawked and roosters shrieked. The two men turned to look at him as he reached the foot of the stairs. He asked, "What is it? What's happened?" He looked up at one, then the other. "It's my boy, isn't it?"

"Yes, sir." The older man removed his cap. "I'm Chaplain Michael Page, and this is Sergeant David Wilkerson."

The smooth-cheeked Sergeant took off his cap, coughed, and ran his fingers through the inch-long stubble on his head.

The chaplain said, "We regret to inform you that First Lieutenant Benjamin Jorgenson was involved in an accident yesterday." He paused and then said, "May we come in? Ma'am? Sir?"

Carol stood aside. The three men filed in.

"He's not dead," Elmer said as he pulled the door shut and turned to face everyone. It was not a question.

"Yes, sir," the chaplain said solemnly. "I am so sorry."

Elmer didn't let go of the doorknob. He found he couldn't catch his breath with lungs burning and his heart exploding in his ribcage. Carol reached out and clutched his arm, and for a moment, her grip was all that kept Elmer from fainting. For a moment he felt only the tightening on his forearm, and then they both stumbled forward to sit together on the sofa. Elmer gestured for the men to sit down. Carol's hand found his.

"What happened?" Carol choked out as tears rolled down her cheeks. "What in the world happened?"

"Your son and two other soldiers were driving a transport vehicle carrying heavy equipment and first aid supplies," the chaplain said. "A tire blew out, and they ran off the road into a gully. Equipment shifted forward and struck all three men. The other two men were badly bruised, but your son received a blow to the back of the head. It was a freak accident."

"A bump on the head?" Elmer asked. "How can that kill somebody? Are you sure there hasn't been a mistake? Ben has the hardest head in the family. He's been thrown by horses, clobbered by machinery—once he even hit his head when he fell out of the hay loft. Are you sure it's him?" Elmer's eyes pleaded into those of the older soldier.

"It is your son, Mr. Jorgenson," Chaplain Page said. "I'm really sorry."

"Did you know our boy? Either of you?" Elmer asked, as he looked from one to the other.

"No, sir, I didn't," the younger man mumbled.

"But I had met him, sir," Chaplain Page said. "I had the privilege of meeting him and several of his buddies at the chapel service in Wheaton last August when he was called up for Operation Desert Shield."

Elmer heard a tiny knock at the door. For a moment, the sound didn't register, then he rose, and went to open the front door. Nealy stood on the top stair holding the kite and a tangle of string. The kite's tail was knotted and twisted. He stared down at her, wordlessly, and she peered up at him wide-eyed and curious. "I'm going home now, Mr. J." she finally said.

"Yes, Nealy. Goodbye." He shut the door.

The chaplain and soldier stayed for almost two hours. They offered to help with arrangements and to make telephone calls, and before they left, Chaplain Page said he would be back when Ben's body was shipped in.

Carol called their other two children, Donna and Mary, and she told Elmer they were on their way down from Fargo. He heard her tearful calls to her sisters and to his older brothers and younger sister. He sat silent in his chair. He was sure he hadn't taken a breath in the last two hours. He imagined he was dreaming as he looked out across his wheat fields and saw himself slumped over the wheel of the tractor tilling a row straight from his heart across the Minnesota border and into nearby South Dakota.

Elmer sat stone-faced for the remainder of that week and into the next. He heard his wife's sobs, saw the grief-filled faces of her sisters and his own siblings. He accepted hugs and handshakes and words of consolation. He listened to friends and neighbors reminisce about all the funny things Ben had said and done. But little penetrated. His inmost self had turned to petrous stone, except for the furnace burning in his chest, an anger burning bright as a flash fire. He forced himself to sit silent for fear that his rage would come out in a torrent, engulfing everyone around him. He found he could not speak, could not eat. He hardly breathed. *Ben is dead. Ben is dead? My son can't be dead. Why, we just got his latest letter last week. He said he was so hungry in Saudi Arabia:*

> *"...Instead of Desert Shield, this military operation should be called Dessert Congealed. I'm so sick of sweetened canned fruit. I'm craving a piece of your chocolate cake, Mom. And a decent roasted chicken, not this pasty pressed junk..."*

Elmer knew some passages in the letter by heart. He read all his son's letters many times, and he'd shared parts of that one with friends and neighbors who loved to hear his funny descriptions. Always cutting up, unlike his older sisters who were much more serious. Of course, all three children had made it through college, Mary and Donna in business, and Ben in agriculture. Then the girls both married and moved up to the city, but not Benny.

After fall harvest, he'd said, "Dad, I'm joining the Army."

"The Army? Why would you want to do that? I thought you wanted to farm with me."

"Oh, I do. Nothing I like better than farming and raising animals, but I want to see the world. Meet new people. Sow some wild oats, unfamiliar ones, I mean." He smiled and winked at Elmer. "You know how Uncle Tom always talks about how great it was in the Second World War, how he traveled, saw things, and met all those great buddies. I want to try that out."

"The war was not a good time, Ben. Uncle Tom exaggerates. I lost so many cousins in that war. God, it was awful. I don't even like to think about it."

"I know, Dad. I know. But we're not in a war. Peace is breaking out all over the world. Look at the Berlin Wall and the president playwright of Czechoslovakia. Look what's happening now in Poland. It's amazing. The world is changing, and I want to see some of it."

Elmer wanted to argue, but he saw that dreamy, set look in his son's eyes and knew it would be of no use. Ben always had to find things out for himself. Elmer closed his eyes and shook his head in exasperation.

"Dad. Don't be a Father Fudd now." Ben took hold of Elmer's forearm. "Don't worry. When you want to kick back in a few more years, let me know, and I'll be back to take over the farm in an instant."

Ben was called up after the new year, and following initial orientation, he was sent to Germany and later was transferred to Saudi Arabia.

Elmer had begun to look forward to his son's permanent return, especially after Ben wrote that he didn't like the bureaucracy and rigidity of military life. Before the Iraqis invaded Kuwait, he wrote:

> *"Are you ready for me to come home next summer? I'm wanting to start building a place of my own at the end of the lane by the crick. Better start laying in supplies, Dad. I've got huge plans..."*

Only Ben shared Elmer's love of farming. As children, Mary enjoyed raising and riding horses, and Donna dutifully milked the cows and collected the eggs, but their interests lay elsewhere. Elmer's two older children were both happy living in the city. Ben was different. He shared Elmer's passion for the land. He believed in caring for the farm and animals and wanted to pass along his ideas and theories about farming to others. He belonged to the Future Farmers of America and Ducks Unlimited. He loved 4-H and threw himself into projects with a zest most adults lacked.

4-H was responsible for the family's introduction to kiting. When he was twelve, Ben went to 4-H Nationals in Washington, D.C. Elmer and Carol escorted Ben to the East Coast, and it was near the Washington Monument that Elmer caught sight of twenty or thirty multi-colored kites wafting in the wind. Some were simple bow kites, but others were large hexagonal boxes, octagonal wheels, or complicated bat-like para-wings. The World Kite-Fliers Association was in town, sponsored by the Smithsonian, and Ben could not have been happier. He was fascinated to hear their names: the Edo Yakko, the USA Starflake, the Weifang Butterfly, the famous fighter kite of India called the Tukkal Star, and the Bali Giants. He wanted to know everything immediately and asked the kiters so many questions Elmer worried they'd think his son a nuisance. The kiters enjoyed the boy and his excitement, and they promised to put him on their mailing list.

The packet from the Kite-Fliers Association arrived a week after Ben returned home. From the initial information, Elmer and Ben ordered a kite-making kit and began to learn how to build them. At first, they decorated white plastic garbage bags with permanent markers to make the kites' skin. They used eighth-inch dowels for the spars and experimented with nails, glue, tape, and staples to fasten the paper or plastic to the kite frames. Soon they became more adventurous. Elmer bought expensive strips of spruce, and Carol showed Elmer and Ben how to sew skins from silk and lightweight cloth. The silk-skinned Eddy kite was their crowning achievement and was the envy of Ben's schoolmates.

Even after Ben got older and lost interest in kite-making, Elmer took time every year to visit schools and teach children how to make and fly kites. He became the region's kite expert, a distinction bringing him considerable popularity with elementary school teachers and principals.

The phone rang and startled Elmer out of his memories. He heard Carol answer.

"Elmer," Carol said. "Nealy is wondering if she could come over to fly kites for a while."

"No," he said. "No. I can't." He rose from his chair, stumbled through the kitchen and out the back door, and went into the barn by the woodpile. He took his favorite axe down off the rack and set up a chunk of tree to split. When he got tired, he sat down on the worn wheel of his father's prize tractor, a rusty red 1928 International Harvester F-14.

"Elmer."

He turned to see Carol outlined in the doorway of the barn, but he stayed seated on the tractor wheel. "I've been calling you for dinner," she said. She came to him and leaned into his arms. As she pressed against him, he sighed and let his face rest against her green sweater.

When she stepped back from the hug and looked into his face, he stood and reached behind him to touch the slotted metal seat of the ancient tractor. "They don't make things like this anymore, Carol."

"Yes, you're right."

"Nowadays," he said with a choke, "F-14's aren't for farming. They're for killing." He turned his face from her. She stepped back toward him, but he turned and inched away.

She took hold of his arm and said, "I miss him, too, Elmer. It hurts my heart to think of it." Her eyes brimmed with tears.

He didn't know what to say. He turned from her and walked toward the house, and she followed in silence. He sat at the table and pushed the food around on his plate.

As she put a small second helping of mashed potatoes and gravy on her plate, Carol said, "El, honey, you've got to eat."

"No!" He startled her to tears. "I just can't. I'm not . . . not hungry." He rose suddenly and left the table. He felt Carol's eyes on him, knew her sadness, too. He saw her tears, had listened to her sobs in the night, but he found himself turning away, curling up within himself. He grabbed his jacket, left the kitchen, and walked aimlessly about the farm in the deepening twilight of the Hunter's Moon.

Elmer remembered earlier days on the farm right after his parents died. Ben, Mary, and Donna were nine, ten, and twelve. First, Elmer's mother died of cancer; then a year later his father was exposed to a lethal dose of nitrogen gas from a leaky fertilizer tank. He died two days later.

Elmer remembered his sadness and confusion. He feared he could not run the farm alone. Carol fretted that bad things happened in threes, and Elmer hoped losing the farm was not the third event.

It was a lean year. Crops were scarce due to drought. In frustration, some nights Elmer shot at deer to keep them away from the corn crib, not to mention the cherry tree in the front yard. Nine-year-old Ben watched the deer, saw their gaunt figures and wounded eyes. "Dad, couldn't we feed those deer? Why do you gotta shoot at them and scare 'em away? They're just hungry."

"We will be, too, Ben. If it was hunting season, I'd take 'em down. As it is, we hardly have enough feed for the pigs and cows. Can't afford to feed all these deer too."

Ben was not satisfied with Elmer's explanation. He left the lid to the corn crib up more than once, and he managed to drop—accidentally, of course—table scraps and hog feed around the barnyard. Elmer was both irritated and amused. Then one dusky fall afternoon, he came back from duck hunting in the slough. He turned the south corner of the cavernous red barn and saw his son holding out half an apple to a mother deer. A tiny spindly-legged fawn stood twenty feet away.

"Ben! No!"

At that instant, the deer started as she took hold of the apple and part of Ben's hand. She bit down. Ben cried out as the animal leapt, turned, and bounded away.

Elmer groped for the rifle trigger and shot, then stumbled toward his son as the deer pitched forward into the fading light and collapsed next to the chicken house. The little fawn followed and nuzzled at her mother's heaving body.

Elmer set the gun on a bale of hay and turned to his son. He found Ben down on his knees, blood spreading over the knees of his bib overalls. "Benny! Benny! Are you all right?"

"No, Dad. She bit me. But she didn't mean to do it. You scared her."

Elmer examined Ben's hand and saw two jagged, half-moon tears in Ben's forefinger and palm. He pulled out his handkerchief and wrapped it around his son's hand. "How many times have I told you that wild animals are dangerous?"

Ben winced with pain as his father helped him to his feet. He stood, a little unsteady, and said, "But Dad, I've fed her before, and she never bit me. If you hadn't come, she'd have been fine."

"Come on. We have to get you into town. A doctor is going to have to look at this."

The trip to town was just the beginning of Ben's ordeal. The Wheaton General Clinic didn't have the surgical facilities for a delicate operation on tendons and fingers. After the Wheaton practitioner wrapped the hand and gave the boy a painkiller, an ambulance drove Ben and Carol all the way to St. Luke's Hospital in Fargo where his palm was operated on and sutured. Elmer had to go back to get the dead deer so that it could be tested for rabies.

When Elmer arrived back at the farm, he found the fawn was dead, too. She was pressed so tightly against the mother that at first Elmer thought the mother must have rolled over on her baby. As he drew closer, he realized that the fawn's small frame was emaciated. Likely she starved to death in just the last few hours. The mother's hide was mottled with sores and infested. Elmer was glad Ben was not there to see this sight. He dragged the fawn over behind the storage shed so he could bury her later. Then he loaded the mother deer into the bed of the truck and drove to Fargo.

Ben got injections to guard against tetanus, and he was lucky the deer didn't have rabies. He stayed in the hospital two nights. At first, doctors worried the bite might have damaged the tendons of his finger, but Ben healed up quickly after the surgery, and his fingers were back to normal in a few weeks.

Elmer knew Ben could have died from the deer bite, but at the time, he tried not to think about it. Ben was always getting into things and banging himself up—much like Elmer had as a child. Now when he looked back, he wondered why his son had lived through that and died over a bump on the head. "God," he asked out loud, "Why? Why, did you save my boy then, only to take him away now?" Elmer stood staring into the empty corncrib and cried bitter tears.

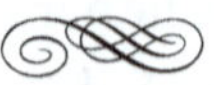

Eight long days later, Ben's remains arrived at the mortuary in town. The funeral was on an ash-gray November morning. Folks estimated that nearly everybody in town attended. All the farm families from miles around came, and there was a contingent of young Lakota men Ben had known through the stewardship projects he worked on. Elmer passed the morning nodding, shaking hands, unable to speak. His throat hurt, and everything seemed blurry. The only clear moment occurred when he finally set eyes on his boy lying so still in the casket, eyes closed, hands folded, his dress uniform looking crisp and regal.

Why, there isn't even a scratch on him, Elmer thought. *Not a single scratch.* He resisted the strong urge to reach into the casket and turn Ben's hand over just to make sure the old suture marks were still there. Though he couldn't see the fingers of Ben's hand, the scar that curled near Ben's right knuckle was plain. Elmer gave up all hope that there might have been a mix-up in identifying Ben. There was no mistaking his son.

A week after the funeral, three letters arrived from Ben's Army buddies. Two were brief notes of sympathy, awkwardly written and phrased. The third was different and Elmer read and re-read it.

> *Dear Mr. and Mrs. Jorgenson,*
>
> *How are you? I am fine. I'm real sorry for your loss. I was there in the truck when it happened, and I still can't believe it. One minute we were talking about girls and hunting and kites. The next minute somebody lowered a ton of bricks. I don't know why it was the Lieutenant and not me. I got nothing to live for, no home to go back to. I barely even graduated from high school. Don't get me wrong—I'm grateful to be alive, but I can't help believing it was unfair that your son would be the one.*

Seems like I'm not making sense, but what I mean is I'll miss Ben. He was like a big brother to me and besides, he told good jokes.
Yours Truly,
Vaughn Meechem, PFC

Elmer went back to the beginning of Private Meechem's letter and read it again. In each reading he searched for something, a clue, a message, some matter of importance. But he discovered nothing and found himself wondering what he expected from a nineteen-year-old boy.

Finally he got up from the living room chair and went outside. He walked past the barn and looked around. He saw the maple tree with the three-story treehouse. Ben had wanted to leave it up for his children. Next to the empty hog pen, Elmer noticed the leaning doghouse Donna and Ben had built. They hadn't owned a dog for several years, and the roof was falling into disrepair. Past the barn he saw the hillock the kids always took sleds down in the winter. The gusting breeze chilled him, and as he listened closely to the wind, he could almost hear the wild hoots and excited shouts of his three children playing in the distance.

Soon it grew dark. With lips chapped and his body cold clear through, Elmer went inside to another sleepless night.

The roof to the storage shed still leaked, and Elmer needed more tar. He'd left the last tube in the caulking gun on the roof, and it had dried up. He got in his weathered Chevy truck and drove into town.

It was a busy day in Wheaton, even with the cold blustery wind and the threatening storm clouds. The grocery store parking lot was half-full, and three men from church stood talking in front of the bar next to the hardware store. Elmer drove by, went up to the corner, and rounded the block. He took his time, and when he turned back onto Main Street, the men were waving at one another and getting into their trucks. He parked in front of Irma's New and Used Shop. When he got out of the truck, the first thing he saw was a red, white, and blue bumper sticker on a Ford Bronco that read: *Don't Let the Bully of Baghdad Kick Sand in Our Face.* He wheeled away and headed toward the Ace Hardware.

"Hey, Elmer, old buddy," someone said, grasping Elmer's arm and turning him around. Elmer frowned and focused in on the face of his neighbor, Nealy's father. The man reached for Elmer's hand and shook it while patting Elmer on the shoulder. "Good to see you, Elmer."

"Hi, Marvin."

"Haven't seen you down at the bowling alley in a while. Must be going on three, four weeks. We've missed you."

Elmer didn't say anything, just nodded.

Marvin said, "Why don't you come have a bite to eat with me? I'll treat."

Elmer didn't like the way Marvin looked at him. He thought he saw pity in his eyes. "No, thanks, Marv. I've got to pick up some supplies and get back before it sleets or snows." He turned and started to walk away.

"Whoa, Elmer. Hold up. Come on in and talk with me. I know just how you feel. I lost my father a couple years ago, and it's awful."

Elmer clamped his lips shut and glared at his neighbor. He wanted to say, "It isn't the same. You've never lost a son, a child. Nealy and your three boys are fine. You don't know what it's like. You damn well *can't* know!" He looked down, then cleared his throat as if to speak, but all that came out was a coughing sound. He let the sound trail off and again turned to leave.

"Wait, Elmer. I just gotta say one more thing." Elmer half turned to look back, but he kept on walking. "We're going to kick Iraq's butt. That's what we'll do. They'll pay, you know." Marvin stood, feet apart, one fist shaking in the air. His graying hair hung in a limp half-circle around his face as he shook his head. The last thing Elmer heard him shout was, "I'm confident, Elmer. We're gonna do it for Ben."

Elmer pulled his collar up and jammed his hands into the scratchy wool pockets of his old plaid coat. He leaned into the blasting wind, which pinched tears out of the corner of his eyes, and walked on.

The town was four blocks long, four and a half on one side counting the bowling alley with the Elks Lodge attached. The post office across the street, constructed of solid stones mortared together, was the oldest building in town. Out front, the flag whipped in the wind, half wrapped around the flagpole. The red and white stripes jerked and twisted in the breeze. Elmer looked away and glanced into the Tubs of Grunge Laundromat where he saw two young men standing over a basket of knotted clothes. They laughed and pointed at something in the basket. Elmer walked on.

All along the street, he looked in shop windows and saw people working, talking, shopping, moving with purpose. He marveled at their energy. He caught the scent of bacon as he moved past Holly's Diner. For a moment he considered going in for a cup of coffee, but just then, a waitress looked out and saw him. She smiled and waved, and she looked so happy to see him that it was all he could do to grimace back, wave, and turn away.

Walking quickly, he traveled back a block and went into the hardware store where he bought two tubes of black tar. He was thankful he did not recognize the gum-snapping young man behind the cash register.

Later, when Elmer thought he had tarred the roof enough to seal the leaks, he threw away the used tube and cleaned his hands with solvent until they were red and sore. He'd heard Carol call him in for supper earlier, so he closed up the storage shed and went in the house.

The dawn sky was pink and red when Elmer rose. He pulled coveralls on over his long johns and picked up his socks and work boots. He tiptoed out of the room, leaving Carol sleeping. Leaning against the kitchen counter, he drank a cup of cold coffee, then put on his socks, boots, and coat, all the while surveying the gun rack. He took down Ben's ten-gauge shotgun.

Silently, he left the house and began to pick his way toward the slough. He walked along frost-covered ruts of plowed field for half a mile and through knee-high wheat until he reached a place where broken and leaning rushes began to appear. He crawled through a rusty barbed wire fence and followed the worn trail to the slough. Here and there on the thin ice, he saw muskrat houses built up from mounds of mud and sticks. Lately, there had been severe windstorms, so the surface of the slough water had frozen in odd rippled patterns. Elmer resisted the urge to take the short cut across the expanse of white ice. The slough was never more than three feet deep, but if he broke through in his low leather boots, he knew it would be excruciatingly cold, so he hugged the edges.

Elmer looked back to see the farmhouse his father had built. A mile away, it looked so cozy with the sun coming up behind it in the rose and baby blue colored sky. *What will become of it when Carol and I are gone?* "There's no one left," he whispered. "No one."

He pushed forward, looking for the low duck stand he'd built the fall before and found it nearly grown over with weeds. The posts and supporting boards were sticking up, but the platform had disappeared completely. *Must have been some kind of windstorm.*

He stood gazing around the open prairie, as the wind in his face brought tears to his eyes. Far away, a shot rang out. He envisioned rifle-bearing hunters in fluorescent orange taking potshots at everything that moved, and he hunched over and looked around. Then, without warning, a vision came to him of Ben inching along in the sand on his belly while Iraqi soldiers fired guns and dropped chemical bombs. It was more than Elmer could bear. He sank down to the thin crossboard of the duck stand and began to sob. *Oh, Benny. Ben, I've lost you to an enemy I couldn't even imagine. An accident. A damnable accident. It wasn't even enemy fire. Just a stupid, unfortunate accident.*

A mile away, another shot rang out, and this time a flock of pheasants nearby spooked and flapped upwards. From his seated position, Elmer automatically pulled Ben's gun to his shoulder, squinted into the sight, and paused. Much to his surprise, he found he couldn't pull the trigger. The birds flew back behind his line of vision and were gone, but Elmer continued to peer through the sight. Then, with a long sigh, he leaned the gun against the wooden stand.

He shuddered. Quietly he whispered, "I don't think I'll ever kill another living thing again. I just can't do it."

His eyes filled with tears, which trickled down his face. He sat for a very long time, weeping in silence, then wiped his face on the dusty sleeve of his work jacket and wept some more. Each time the tears subsided, they returned as fiercely as before. For a good hour he sat until he was so cold he thought his whole body must be blue.

Elmer rose and wiped his tears away. He put his hands into his jacket pockets and turned to face the shelterbelt of trees surrounding his house. Hovering above the trees, he was surprised to see a silver, black and red object flashing and luminous in the early morning sun. Far away, near the storage shed, he saw a red dot, a tiny figurine. Next to the spot of red, he recognized the brown-clad figure of his wife, twice the size of Nealy.

Carol's arm moved in a rolling motion as she and Nealy stepped toward one another, backed away, shifted again, coordinating their reels of invisible string. The proud Eddy kicked and wheeled, tossing and dancing in the air, its silver tail whipping in the wind.

Elmer stood watching for several minutes. He wiped his eyes once more, then stepped over a muskrat mound and picked his way back around the slough. Keeping an eye on the kite, he strode carefully through the ice and rushes and leaning wheat, onward to his wife, to his young friend, to the warmth of the farmhouse, and to the sorrow he must share.

Everything You Learn in Kindergarten Can Ruin Your Life

With Apologies to Robert Fulghum

Even twenty years after leaving kindergarten, Dross Point Elementary had changed little. I walked the deserted playground, and looked into the windows of the ground floor classrooms, remembering. The same sign with the same rules for successful navigation through kindergarten waters was posted in big block letters next to the schoolhouse door above a wooden platform. Back when I attended Dross Point, the table below contained three cages labeled Mice, Snake, and Bunny. The cages were gone, but the rules remained:

1.   *Share and play fair.*
2.   *Don't hit.*
3.   *Clean up after yourself or ask for Teacher's help.*
4.   *Don't take others' things.*
5.   *Say you're sorry and shake hands when you hurt somebody.*
6.   *When Teacher says to line up, hold hands and stick together.*

Seeing that worn placard was all it took to transport me back to those days. The rules . . . six easy rules. Trouble was, I must have been the only child able to read.

The first day of kindergarten, as soon as my mother settled me in a desk, kissed my forehead twice, and left, a blond girl in a cutesy-pie, polka-dotted, lace-trimmed dress sidled up to me and knocked me out of the chair with a well-timed hip roll.

"This is *my* chair," she said.

I looked up at her from my reclining position on the wood floor as she sat down in my chair, and I started to protest. "Hey! The rules say—" I stopped. The rules didn't cover this incident. They said not to hit, but she hadn't actually hit me. She'd "nudged" me, and done it in such a way that even the teacher, Mrs. Floyd, didn't notice. What Mrs. Floyd did see was me sprawled on the floor, my plaid gingham dress up around my waist so every little boy in the room could see the seams of my white leotards.

"What's your name?" the teacher asked.

"Allison Bowler," I told her as I scrambled to my feet.

"Well, Allison, quit messing around and pay attention." She turned to the roomful of children milling around and said, "Everyone line up: girls on the left, boys on the right. Before it starts to rain again, we're going to have a walking tour of your section of the playground. Then we will come back in and get to work." She clapped her hands together and made clucking noises.

I reached for the hand of the girl next to me. It was Miss Cutesy Pie.

She pushed me and said, "Ick. Get away from me." In a loud, plaintive voice she said, "Teacher, she's bothering me again."

"Allison," Mrs. Floyd said. "Get to the end of the line."

"But . . . but the rules said—"

"Hush now and do as I say," the teacher said.

I went to the end of the line and stood next to a tiny, dark-skinned girl in jeans and a red sweater. She had soft, black hair and large eyeglasses, and she stared downward at her red bumper toe sneakers. I said hello to her, but she didn't answer.

The teacher went down the rows, asked all twenty-four of us our names, and pinned sticky nametags to our chests. The tiny child next to me was Emma. Miss Cutesy-Pie was named Leanna.

Dross Point Elementary was an immense brick building flanked on either side by two freestanding portable classrooms. The playground spread out on three sides around the buildings, with the fourth side fenced off due to the busy street. We stood near Mrs. Floyd as she pointed to a large concrete section of the schoolyard containing a jungle gym, swings, painted grids for playing Four-Square, and metal bars to twirl on.

"This is your side of the playground," Mrs. Floyd said. "Only kindergarten and first graders are allowed into this area. You will be punished if you go beyond that gate." She gestured toward a chain-link fence and gate just past the portable classroom.

Two of the boys behind me jostled one another.

"Stop that!" Mrs. Floyd said, shaking her finger at the group of us. "I won't stand for it. If you don't behave, there will be no Recess or Play Time for you. Now come along. Let's get back inside, and I'll assign your desks and explain the rules."

The mornings I spent at school dragged slowly for me. I was happy to see the colorful books, toys, stuffed animals, and chalkboards, but I felt out of place. Perhaps it was because I entered kindergarten almost a year later than most children. My father had worked out of town for the entire previous year, and Mama and I shuttled eight hundred miles back and forth between the house in St. Paul and a tiny, cramped apartment in Montana.

For the first several weeks of school, I went home feeling great relief at having escaped. I didn't even mind Mama keeping me in a lot and forcing me to be a solitary child. She hated it when I played with the neighbor boys who she said were mean and dirty, and she didn't want me to catch cold. So I learned to read early and spent my time by myself playing with Legos, Tinker Toys, and coloring books.

Each day at school, we had to choose an activity for Play Time: building blocks, finger-painting, playing house, making desk tents, reading storybooks, drawing at our desks, or playing "Chutes and

Ladders" with two sixth graders who came in for half an hour each day. By the second week, I dreaded it. How could I avoid Cutesy-Pie Leanna, not to mention many of the other children who were rambunctious, mean and mouthy? Usually I chose reading, but after a solid week of hiding in the corner with storybooks on a large pillow, Mrs. Floyd noticed.

"Allison Bowler, you need to do more than read. Today you should—" she squinted down at her list "—play house with Merle and Leanna."

A burning sensation in my chest radiated in my chest, and it hurt to breathe. Mrs. Floyd ushered me over to the false front of the playhouse. It had no roof, but there was a squatty red front door, hardly taller than I was. On either side of the door were windows with no panes. The left window looked into a sitting area, and the right one into the kitchen.

"Teacher," I asked, "why isn't there a bathroom or bedroom in this little house?"

"Oh, Allison, what a foolish question. Go in now and play." She left me at the doorstep, where I stood poised between entering and fleeing.

I peered through the door and saw a rainbow of clashing color. The kitchen was decked out especially strange. A pink refrigerator and stove sat next to a gray sink made of heavy cardboard. When the sink faucet was turned, strips of tinsel hanging from the spigot twisted and swirled. A two-foot-tall, neon yellow table squatted nearby, surrounded by four one-foot-tall lime green chairs. The white counter was stacked with black plastic pots, orange frying pans, green bowls, a tea set, tiny red and gold serving trays, and miniature silverware. An ironing board and iron stood in the corner, and nearby a pile of baby clothes lay next to a heap of motley-looking dolls. A tiny blue and gold mop and broom set hung from hooks on the wall.

Leanna stood at the sink wearing a black-and-white striped apron with lace around the bottom. She picked up some grimy forks and knives, turned toward the table, and saw me.

"Oh. It's you. Listen up. I'm the Mommy here," she said in a threatening voice as she shook a handful of silverware at me.

"And I'm the Daddy," Merle said from the other room. "So, I guess you'll be our slave. Slave, bring me a beer. And wife, get the dinner on the table."

"Yes, dear," Leanna said.

Beer? I thought. *They've got beer?* Leanna rushed past me and handed "Daddy" an empty Yogi Bear cup. He pretended to drink from it, making a loud slurping noise, then set it down on the floor below his chair.

Merle sat sideways on a tattered paisley wingback chair. His legs lapped over one of the chair's arms, his neck against the other arm, and his hands were laced behind his head. I stepped through the kitchen and into the sitting room area. A black box with a blue-colored screen and no legs sat on the floor. The fake-looking knobs drawn on it were purple. On a wooden table next to Merle was an orange plastic lamp with a papier-mâché shade.

From above, I searched for a switch, but couldn't see one. I noticed there was no light bulb in it, anyway.

"Daddy, dear," Leanna said. "Come to dinner now."

Merle rose and pushed past me. He sat in one of the green chairs and said, "Smells good. What's for dinner tonight?"

"Ice cream, chocolate sauce, nuts, bananas, cherries, and whipped cream."

"All right!" he shouted. He pounded on the rickety table as he laughed with glee.

"And there are Oreo cookies for dessert," she said.

Merle picked up his fork and pretended to eat from the tiny silver-and-white plate. I decided to join him and pulled out a tiny green chair.

"What do you think you're doing?" Leanna asked.

"Yeah," Merle growled out. He had a very deep voice for a six-year-old.

"You aren't allowed to eat until you've done your work," Leanna said, "Look at all that ironing you have to do." She kicked at the stack of baby clothes. "Besides, the children will eat before you do." She grabbed the bedraggled foot of a nearly bald doll wearing only a sack dress and tossed it toward me. "No food for you until the house is clean and all the laundry is done."

She and Merle giggled and made faces at me. I stood, fists clenched, and tried not to cry. I wanted to push them out of their chairs and hit them. I thought of poking out their eyes with the miniature cutlery, and then I heard *ding-ding-ding*. Mrs. Floyd rang the bell to tell us Play Time was over.

"Return to your desks, children," she said in a warbly voice as she clapped her hands together.

My two friends were Joey, a boy who stuttered, and Emma, the quiet, black girl with quarter-inch-thick glasses. I towered over both of them. I was the tallest child in the class, though Merle was only an inch shorter and probably doubled me in weight. He said naughty words when the teacher wasn't listening, and his bullying ways frightened Joey, Emma, and me.

One overcast winter day at Recess, Joey waved to Emma and me and said, "C-c-c-come over here. I'll show you something."

Emma and I followed him around the side of the brick building away from teacher's eyes. He reached into the pocket of his oversized coat and pulled out a shiny black plastic pistol.

"Wow," I said in admiration. Emma stared at it and nodded while keeping her hands in her pockets.

I reached for the gun. "Can I see?"

"Sure."

It felt heavier than the neighbor boys' cap pistols.

"Look," Joey said. "There's a sp-sp-sp-special loading thing in the handle." He took it and showed me how a cartridge popped in and out of the gun butt. "That doesn't make the shooting sound though," he said. "A cap deal goes in the side here. But I don't h-h-have any right now." He opened another compartment and started to hand the gun to me.

I was so intent that I paid no attention to Emma's sudden intake of breath.

"What are you little weenies doing?" Merle said as he loomed over the three of us.

I saw Joey's eyes go wide, and he let go of the pistol. I fumbled for a moment but managed to keep it from falling to the ground. Emma backed up as Merle took hold of Joey's coat lapel and pushed him against the brick wall.

"Dopey, dopey, dopey," Merle whined in a falsetto voice as he pushed against Joey. Emma turned and ran. Joey's face was white, and he tried to speak, but only a choking noise came out.

"Let him go," I said. I held the black gun up to Merle's head and cocked the trigger.

Merle swung Joey by his arm in a half-circle and tossed him flat on his stomach ten feet away, then turned and grinned at me. He snatched the gun out of my hand. I put my head down and plowed into him, but I bounced back and he laughed.

"Where'd you get this?" he said.

"None of your business. It's not yours. Give it back!"

I pushed at him and tried to reach for it. By then, Joey was up and standing near. Merle held the gun away from me and above his head with his left hand. Without warning, he socked me in the stomach and in one fluid motion, hit me in the head with the gun.

"Girls don't play with guns," he hissed as he turned and ran around the corner.

I had a funny metallic taste in my mouth and a creeping sensation on my forehead. Joey was reaching for my arm when Mrs. Floyd came around the corner dragged by Emma.

"Joey Burr," Mrs. Floyd shouted. "What have you done to Allison?"

"N-n-n-noth-ing."

She came to me and put a handkerchief against my brow. "What happened here?" Mrs. Floyd asked.

"I-I-I . . ." Joey stuttered.

"It was Merle," Emma said. "He was beating up Joey." She paused. "And Allison, too, I guess."

Mrs. Floyd took me into the classroom bathroom and made me sit on the edge of the one-foot-tall children's toilet while she washed out the cut on my brow and put a big bandage on it. Emma and Joey hovered outside the door.

"What did you do to provoke this, young lady?"

"Nothing."

"You must have done something."

"No, I didn't." She kept asking me questions, but I refused to answer.

When asked, Merle lied. He said he ran into Joey and me by accident. He convinced Mrs. Floyd he hadn't meant it. She told him he had to apologize and shake my hand as the rules required.

I couldn't believe it.

"It's the rules, Allison," Mrs. Floyd said.

"He did it on purpose. He should be punished," I said, nearly yelling.

"Oh, come now. He wants to say he's sorry. Let bygones be bygones."

I didn't know what bygones were, but when Merle extended his dirty paw toward me with a smirk on his face, I knew I had no choice but to walk away.

"Allison Bowler. How rude," Mrs. Floyd said. "No Play Time for you today."

Secretly, I cheered.

Emma and Joey talked with me the next day at Recess. We all agreed school was unfair and adults were stupid.

"How are we going to get your gun back, Joey?" I asked.

He shrugged and said, "I don't know. I guess it's g-g-gone."

"There has to be a way," Emma said, more sureness in her voice than usual.

"We can't beat him up," Joey said.

"I bet we could—together, I mean," I told them.

We all looked at each other, and Emma and Joey shook their heads. "No," Emma said. "We'd just get in more trouble, or else he'd hurt us real bad. Mrs. Floyd would be too mad. It's against the rules, you know."

"How come everyone else isn't following the rules, just us?" I asked. I wanted to scream. I kicked a rock thirty-five feet. It would have kept going, except it ran up against the cement retaining wall surrounding our section of the playground.

One Friday night, I walked home with Emma. I had permission to eat supper with her and her little sister. Joey walked along with us. He lived two blocks past Emma's house.

"Look," Emma said. "That's Merle Swanson's house."

She pointed to a ramshackle, blue, two-story home with a gabled roof. Strips of fading paint peeled in some sections revealing bone-colored bare wood. Five rickety stairs led up to a porch covered with greasy car parts. The lawn was full of deep puddles and bare grassless spots. Clumps of dead weeds poked out through pieces of trash. Pop cans, sheets of newspaper, and candy wrappers littered the yard. Two lengths of rope hung from the elm, but there was no swing attached.

"What an ugly house," I said.

Emma and Joey nodded.

"Maybe we should go up and knock," I said. "We could tell his mother how he stole your gun."

Just then the front door blasted open and a bundle of brown and gray and flesh shot out, tripped down the stairs, and landed in a lump in the yard. At the door stood a scrawny man in a greasy t-shirt and baggy black pants. He had a cigarette in his mouth and a liquor bottle in his left hand. Making wild gestures with his right hand, he said,

"Don't come back in today. You already ate up everything decent in the house, asshole."

The man exhaled smoke and flicked his cigarette into the yard, then stepped back inside and slammed the door.

The lump got to its feet slowly, as though it were painful. He stood with his back to us for a moment, then put his hands in his pockets and turned. When Merle saw us, his face changed in an instant from sad to mean.

"What are you doing here?" he said as he started toward us. "Whatchu looking at?"

None of us waited to answer. We ran.

When we got to Emma's house and caught our breath, Joey said, "I don't care about the gun anymore. He can k-k-k-keep it."

Soon, Thanksgiving passed, and I turned seven. I invited Joey, Emma, and Emma's little sister, Sally, to my house for cake and ice cream. My mothers' gift to me was a sweater, Joey gave me a Twister game, and Emma and Sally brought me a cowboy gun and holster set. I could see my mother was horrified, but she kept it to herself.

"Our mom didn't want us to get this," Sally said. She giggled and put her little hand over her mouth as though sharing a great secret.

"Nope," Emma said," but I begged and told her you'd always wanted one, so she finally gave in and let us."

I just smiled. I was so happy I kissed Emma. I wore it all day and to bed that night and only took it off once, when we played Twister.

Emma, Joey, and another little girl were playing Four-Square with me. It had rained that morning, and there were puddles all around, though our square was dry. I was glad to be wearing a new pair of black leather boots polished to a shine. If teacher wasn't within eyeshot, I could have had a lot of fun puddle-stomping.

Girls jumped rope, children climbed on the monkey bars, and boys chased each other, keeping Mrs. Floyd very busy.

All over the playground, there was running and screaming, jumping and ball-bouncing. Out of the corner of my eye, I saw Merle's lumbering frame slouch by, and between ball bounces, I watched him. He walked toward the side of the school, though, and I returned my full attention to the game.

I smacked a hard one to Emma, and she lost control of the ball. It rolled past her. We all turned to watch her race after it, and it was then we saw Leanna and Merle around the side of the school by the portable. He yanked on the collar of Leanna's coat as she tried to pull away. I couldn't hear his words, but from his tone, I could tell he was taunting her, and she was crying. I looked for Mrs. Floyd, but she had her back to us, hollering at some boys on the jungle gym.

"Come on, you guys," I said. We started toward the portable. Several other kids jumping rope nearby dropped their ropes and ran after us.

As we drew close, Emma shouted, "Merle! Let her go."

Merle turned with a surprised look on his face and then stuck his tongue out at Emma.

"Whyn't you make me, little shrimp?" He spit toward Emma and wrenched at Leanna's wool coat.

I didn't think. I darted forward and kicked him in the shins with the hard pointy toe of my new boot. It felt so good I kicked him again and pushed him, and he fell down at the edge of a puddle, grabbing at his shins. "Hey! Hey, cut it out. Cut it out!"

I couldn't stop. I peppered his thighs and backside with several more kicks. "You leave us kids alone! You hear? *Stop* picking on us." I punctuated my shouts with a few more solid kicks.

Over the rush in my head, I heard a chorus behind me saying, "Yeah! Quit beating up on us." I stood over him and contemplated jumping on him and pushing his face down into the puddle, but then I got scared and backed up. Merle wore a pained look on his face. Tears welled up in his eyes, and he turned his head away.

"Here comes Mrs. Floyd!" someone said, and everyone scattered, leaving Merle half in a puddle and Leanna with her mouth open and tears still on her face.

I waited all day for Mrs. Floyd to pull me out of class and punish me, but nothing happened. She didn't even look my way. I expected an ambush from Merle, but it never came. Each time I came near him, he squinted and looked away. For the rest of the year, he acted as if I didn't exist, always swaggering off, head down and hands in pockets.

The day after Merle beat up on Leanna, Emma and I raised our hands to play house at Play Time. No one else was interested. We skipped over to the kitchen and rearranged the dishes on the counter and tidied up the mess the last kids had left.

"Who should be who?" I asked.

Emma was serious for a moment. She frowned and said, "I don't want to be the mom *or* the dad. Let's forget about it and just be our own selves."

"Okay! Good idea."

Just then I caught sight of Leanna standing in the doorway in her frilly blue and orange polka-dotted dress. She clashed with the yellow table and lime-green chairs. I looked at Emma and she looked at me, then we stared at Leanna.

"Can I come in?"

I shrugged my shoulders and turned away. So did Emma.

Leanna shuffled in and sat down in one of the little chairs. "Well," she said, "who's the mommy?"

"Nobody," Emma said. "We're not playing that way."

"What? Somebody has to be the mom."

"Oh, yeah?" I asked. "Why?"

She got a very puzzled look on her face. "Why don't you want there to be a mom and dad?"

"Because it's no fun," Emma said, her arms crossed over her chest.

"But that's *how* you play house," she protested.

"So what!" I said. "I'm sick of stupid rules nobody follows, and we're making up our own now. Me and Emma decided how we're going to play, and we were here first. If you want to do it your way, fine, but me and Emma are doing it our way. Right, Emma?"

"Yup."

"Okay," Leanna said in a resigned voice. "What am I supposed to do?"

"Whatever," Emma said. "Here. Take some of these dishes and set the table. We can make dinner and feed the dolls. They're probably awful hungry."

Leanna looked skeptical as she set out the dishes and silverware, but before long she was pretending to iron, dressing the dolls in their pressed clothes, and seating them, two to a chair. She hummed an off-key tune while Emma and I stirred pots on the stove and talked about the fabulous dinner we were creating.

"Is the soup ready yet?" Leanna asked.

I looked over at the table as the blonde girl pushed her beautiful blonde hair out of her eyes. "Not quite," I said.

"The children are starving," she said as she put the last dolly gently in her chair. I stood off to the side, watching a smile spread on Leanna's face and for a moment, I almost liked her.

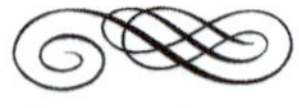

Defending Angels

Jason looked down at the package he found wedged between the screen and front doors. The size of a fat tissue box and with a parcel post stamp emblazoned in red across the front, it was addressed to him. He reached down, picked it up, and shook the package. The corners were slightly damp from the rain seeping in under the poorly fitted screen. He hadn't ordered anything through the mail for a long time and had no idea what it could be.

Tucking the package under his left arm, he shifted his schoolbooks against his left thigh to unlock the front door. He strained to keep hold of his books and the box and wished he had a backpack.

Jason shuffled into the empty house and dumped his books onto the hall table, but he held on to the package and carried it into the small kitchen. Pulling out the breadboard, he set the box down on the few crumbs that lingered from the peanut butter sandwiches his mother had made for him and his two sisters early in the morning.

As usual, his head was throbbing, and the scar running in a diagonal slant from his left part to his right brow was itching again. He leaned against the sink, arms crossed on his chest, and sighed. Then he opened the refrigerator door and surveyed the contents. Not much to choose from: leftover pot roast, carrots and celery, eggs, juice, milk, ketchup, and pickles. He stooped, staring, for at least a minute before shutting the door and walking out of the kitchen to the living room window where he gazed out on the dreary fall day. Cars whisked by. A ratty-looking squirrel darted back and forth from the maple tree to the bushes along the neighbor's walkway. Brown and tan and yellow leaves blew around the yard.

Jason lowered himself across the overstuffed green chair, left shoulder draped over one arm and his right leg over the other arm of the chair. He could see out, but the beige windowsill blocked the view of his yard. He watched the cars speed by and longed for his cinnamon brown Ford Mustang. *Don't think about that. Think about something else.*

Two hours later, Jason awoke to the sounds of the front door opening. His two little sisters bustled into the house followed by his mother, who carried a dripping umbrella and a sack of groceries.

"Hello, Jace," she said. "Can you give me a hand here? Connie and Laura! Get back here on the rug and take those wet shoes off."

Connie rolled her eyes, but kicked her shoes off and ran upstairs. Laura put down her Little Mermaid lunch box and squatted down to unbuckle her shiny black shoes. "Mom! Mom! There's a new girl at daycare," she said, as Jason stepped over her and took the bag from his mother.

"That's nice, dear," Jason heard her say. "Why don't you go get some clean socks on and come down and help me with supper?"

"Okay, Mommy. Then I can tell you all about the new girl. Her name is Tina, and we want to be Barbies for the Halloween party next week."

Jason ignored Laura, stepped over her lunch box and headed for the kitchen. His mother set her umbrella in the rack and followed him. As she turned the corner into the kitchen, she caught sight of the package on the counter.

"What's this, Jason? Looks like you got a package."

"Oh." He paused. "I forgot about that." He picked up the parcel and stared down at it, his hands holding it against his stomach.

"Well, go ahead and open it, dear." She began to put away groceries. Saltine crackers in the cupboard. A package of hot dogs in the fridge. Drano under the sink. She stepped briskly around his tall, rangy figure as she emptied the sack.

Jason fumbled with the package tape and brown paper. Inside he found a sturdy cardboard box, which he opened. In it was a handmade wooden box. He pulled at a tiny pin attached to the box by a chain and popped the hasp open. The wood box was full of taffy and nothing else. He looked at the contents for a moment, and then turned the box over. Picking up the wrapping paper, he asked, "Mom, who do we know from Eden Prairie?"

His mother rinsed her hands in the sink, wiped them off on the towel hanging from the rack by the refrigerator, and came to stand beside him, resting her hand lightly on his shoulder. They both looked down at the mahogany-colored box on the counter.

"I can't think of anyone, Jason. Is there a return address or card?"

"Nope." He selected a red-and-white-striped piece of taffy, twisted open the wax paper ends, and pulled out the candy. He inspected it for a moment, pinched between his thumb and forefinger, before putting it into his mouth. As he chewed it and rolled it around, the taffy softened. He liked the sweet peppermint flavor.

Again, he picked up the brown wrapping, surveying the name on the front: JASON GUNDERSON in bold, block letters. "It's definitely for me. But I wonder who sent it?"

"Perhaps a follow-up letter will arrive in a day or so. Let's wait and see," his mother said.

That night, Jason had the dream again. His hands were strapped behind him, and he sat seat-belted in his Mustang. The car careened along the avenues, skidding and sliding. He tried to press the brake, but his legs would not move. The car went faster and faster until the houses on his right and left were a blur.

Then up ahead he saw the Dutch elm. In the upper branches, his father peered out from the green leaves and waved at him. In one hand, he held a glass from which he sipped as he waved and shouted. Jason felt the car accelerate even more, motor roaring, straight for the tree.

Frantic to get free, he twisted and turned, but he couldn't loosen the tight straps.

"Get down! Run!" he screamed. His father just smiled as he stood on a large lower branch, swigging from his shiny glass. Jason yelled to him one last time, but it was too late. The car struck the tree, and the nose of the Mustang folded in like an accordion. Glass flew, pieces burning into his skin, the fire quenched only by the warm, flowing blood that numbed his body, and obscured his vision.

Jason jerked awake in bed and tried to shake the dream images from his head. In the dark, he could see the outline of his bureau and the hot water radiator at the foot of his bed. On his bedside table, the digital clock read 2:10. Next to the clock, he saw the wooden box. Leaning over, he lifted the lid to take a piece of taffy, then settled back under the covers, sucking on what turned out to be . . . strawberry.

The next package arrived six days later. When he opened the front door after school, Jason saw a small flat packet lying atop the letters stuffed through the mail slot. At first, he thought it was a free sample of laundry soap or pantyhose, but when he picked it up, he saw his name written in the same block letters.

After leaving his books on the hall table, he carried the package into the kitchen, poured himself a glass of milk in a Donald Duck glass, and went into the living room to sit in the rocking chair. He carefully set his glass down on the toy box against the wall and began peeling the tape off the mysterious packet. A folded square of paper and a chain fell out. He picked up the sterling silver chain and saw a ring of shiny silver about an inch in diameter hanging from it. Within the circle was a bird in flight, each of its wings connected to the ring.

Jason picked up his glass of milk, then stared, puzzled, at the necklace. Still gripping the chain, he picked up the paper, unfolded it, and read:

Dear Jason,

I trust the wooden case arrived safely last week. I thought you might like this necklace. In my day, I often wore such a chain. The eagle talisman represents freedom, as well as strength.

From,

Your Guardian Angel

He stared at the note in disbelief, and his hand began to shake so much he almost dropped his glass of milk. He smacked it down on the nearby toy box. *Guardian Angel! There isn't any such thing.* He hadn't believed in heavenly beings for years. He was nine when his next door neighbor, Jimmy, told him all good Catholic children had guardians and prayed to them each day. "O Angel of God, my guardian dear, to whom God's love commits me here, ever this day be at my side, to light and protect, to defend and guide."

Jason was surprised to discover that he still remembered the prayer. Once he believed that he, like Jimmy, was protected by a wonderful winged angel with hair of gold and supernatural powers. That was when he still believed in God.

His chest tightened, and his breathing grew ragged. He fought back tears, hands clutching the rocker arms, as he remembered the house he and his family had lived in on Victoria Avenue near Como Lake. The spacious house had a huge yard and a shabby tool shed out back.

Jason loved to rummage in the shed, nail boards together, and make flat boats that sometimes floated. He hid in the shed whenever he was afraid. Sometimes his little sister, Connie, wandered around the yard calling for him. "Jay-thon? Jay-thon?" He waited until she crawled up the step and over the doorjamb into the shed, and then beckoned her to hide with him under the workbench. Connie thought it was a game as she snuggled up against him in the dusty recesses. She was too young to feel his fright.

Jason's fear became a living, breathing thing with a will of its own the summer after his father lost his job. Profits during the year before had been low, and the foundry laid off three-quarters of its workers just after Christmas. His father was one of many workers never called back when business picked up again. At first, Cliff Gunderson was confident he would be hired elsewhere, but as each day passed, he lost his resolve and became more despondent. He began to go out to the nearby pubs.

After the cold weather passed, Jason's mother took a civil service test and got a job as a clerk in the county's Tax Department. Her husband was furious the day he found out. Jason sat in the breakfast nook on a booster chair eating soup and crackers. He could hear his parents arguing.

His father said, "Give it up. Forget it. No wife of mine needs to work."

"Cliff," she pleaded, "we need the money. Just short-term until you go back to the foundry."

"No way!"

"Your unemployment benefits run out in a few weeks," she reasoned. "The baby and Connie can stay with my sister during the day. If you'll just keep an eye on Jason when he comes home from school, we'll manage. This is only temporary. We *need* the money."

Jason never heard the end of the argument, but his mother continued to work.

In the mornings after his mother left with the girls, Jason watched television and wandered around the house, waiting for his father to wake up. Sometimes before he left for school, he brought his father coffee or juice in bed. It was an excuse to try to waken him. At times, his father was surly and cruel; other times, he was cheerful and drove Jason to school. Jason never knew what to expect.

After school, when Jason got home, his father's friends often came by to take his father to the Snake Eyes Lounge or Smokey Joe's Bar and Grill on Larpenteur Avenue. Jason was on his own then.

At first, Cliff Gunderson was careful to be home before 5:30 when his wife returned from work after picking up the girls. But as spring stretched into summer, he stopped bothering. Some nights he didn't come home at all.

Jason tried not to worry, but his parents argued and fought about money, about household chores, and above all, about his father's drinking. Jason tried not to listen.

Late one night, Jason awakened and heard shouts. His father raged in words Jason couldn't quite make out. He heard his mother's reply in a higher-toned nasal voice. Then they were both shouting at once, and he heard a slap. He leaped out of bed, threw open his door, and raced into the living room.

His father had hold of his mother's arm and curled up his other fist as if to punch her. Jason screamed. He stood in red and blue Superman pajamas, screaming and screaming, fists clenched to his sides, his face white as chalk. His parents gaped at him, motionless, then his father shouted. "Shut up!" and Jason turned and ran.

Eyes wide, gasping for air, he ran down the stairs, out the kitchen door, and tore pell-mell through the backyard. He hit the tool shed door full force, his hands fumbling for the door handle. When the door lurched open, he tripped up the step and fell into the shed. On hands and knees, he scrambled over to the workbench and scooted under, pulling his knees up to his chest and wrapping his arms around them. Shaking, he buried his face into his knees and whispered to himself. "Please, God. Make Daddy stop. I hate this. I hate him. Please fix things. Please, God. Send me my angel. I need one now. Please, God," he sobbed. "Please!"

A noise in the doorway interrupted his prayer, and he turned to see a dark shape bound into the shed. For a moment, he was afraid, but then from the musty fur smell, he knew it was the neighbor's dog. He felt it was a sign, a sign from God. Here was the next best thing to an angel.

"Here, Tippy," he said. "Over here. I'm so glad it's you. Here, girl!"

 Lori L. Lake

Though Tippy was Jimmy's dog, Jason felt like he was part owner. He had gone to the pound with Jimmy's father the day the boys picked out the part German shepherd and part Springer spaniel and took her home. Whenever they slept overnight in the pup tent, the dog stayed with them. When they went to the park to hit baseballs, they took turns pitching to one another, and Tippy brought the outfield hits back to the pitcher's mound.

The dog ambled over to the workbench, licked Jason's bare feet, and laid down against him, snuffling and panting all the while. Jason put his arm around her and felt at peace. He laid his head on the black fur and slept.

It seemed as though he had just drifted off to sleep when a low, steady growl woke him up. Tippy got up on her feet, nose thrust forward, shoulders hunched. Jason heard what Tippy's sensitive ears had already picked up: mumbling and shuffling footsteps. A giant form loomed in the doorway, stepped up and into the shed as Tippy barked fiercely.

"Outta my way, mutt! Where's that boy? Get out from under there." A big hand reached past Tippy and grabbed Jason's foot.

"No, Daddy! Don't!" Jason scrambled back under the farthest corner of the workbench. Tippy barked again and lunged at Jason's father.

"Goddamn mutt!" the big man said as he swatted the dog away. Tippy came back at him, so he aimed a solid kick to her flank. She yelped as he stepped further into the shed. As Tippy jumped at him again, Jason's father tried to steady himself against the bowed, shoulder-high pressboard shelf. There was a snap, and the shelf-support on the left side gave way. A cascade of paint cans, jars of nails and screws, hammers, levels, and a band saw tumbled to the floor.

All was silent for a moment in the dark shed, and then there was a soft whimper. Suddenly Jason launched headlong across the floor.

"Tippy! Tippy, what's wrong?" Jason's hands shoved jars, cans, and tools out of the way in his frantic search for the dog.

"What the hell? What's going on here?" his father asked, his voice gruff and bewildered. He reached above his head, groping for the string hanging from the bulb above, and turned the light on.

"What the hell hap—" He stopped when he saw the animal cradled in his son's arms, with the dog's head hanging at a crooked angle and blood seeping across Jason legs. A can of beige paint had popped open and spattered many of the tools as well as the dog's right paw.

Jason's father turned and shouted, "Sheila! Get out here. Now!"

He stumbled out the door and stepped down, staggering, as his wife rushed from the back porch, across the yard, and past him. She stopped short when she saw her son and Tippy sitting so still in the shed.

Jason's eyes were vacant, though his lips moved. Over and over he muttered, "There is no God. There are no angels. There is no God. There are no angels." He continued to mumble this even after his mother gently removed Tippy from his grasp, picked him up, and held him close.

Now, eight years later, Jason felt the tears welling up in his eyes over this old memory. He didn't want to think about the past anymore. He looked down at the chain and talisman he clutched in his hand. His head was light while his body felt heavy, and his breath came in short wheezes. With a jerk, he pitched the necklace across the room where it hit the bay window and slid down to the sill.

Staring blankly for a moment, he regretted the action, but his head and body felt fused once again. With effort, he got up from the rocker and walked over to the window to get his chain. He stood studying the eagle, and then took it upstairs and put it in the wooden box with the note.

He forgot about his milk.

Nearly a month passed before Jason received another package. This one came on a Saturday.

"Jason," his mother called up the stairs. "You got some mail."

He lay on his bed, knees pulled up, sketch pad resting against his thighs. He was working on an unfinished line drawing of a car. He turned on his side and let the pad slip to the floor to join the jumble of black drawing pencils already there. Then he got up with a weary sigh and went downstairs.

He saw the lettering on the package and halted. Who was doing this? And why?

"Mom, who's this from?" he shouted toward the kitchen.

His mother came around the corner, a wooden spoon in hand and tomato sauce splattered on her apron. The smell of frying hamburger filled the air.

"What is it, son?"

"I don't know," he said with irritation in his voice.

"Go on and open it then. Maybe this time there is a return address or a clue."

He opened the end of the package and pulled at the box inside. He had to rip the brown paper and tug three ways before got it out and found a model kit of the *Spirit of St. Louis,* 276 pieces, complete with a small Lindbergh pilot dressed in brown and wearing an aviator earflap cap. There was no note.

Jason felt his mother's eyes boring into him, and he flushed as he turned to face her. "Do you think Dad is doing this? He can't possibly be trying to . . . to—"

"To make up with you?" his mother asked. Jason's set jaw and downcast eyes furnished his reply.

"Well, dear, he's still in jail, and he probably won't be getting out for several months. Somehow, I don't think he could be sending these things. And there's no note again, for the second time?"

Jason stared at his mother for a moment and then said, "Oh, I never told you; I got another gift a few weeks ago with a note. Signed 'Your Guardian Angel.' The present was a necklace. Here—I'll get it for you." He walked up the stairs to his room and returned a minute later with the wooden box. Setting it on top of the model, he opened the lid.

There were only a few pieces of taffy left, along with the note and the chain. He handed his mother the note, and she read it. Then they looked at one another, puzzled.

"Let me dump this spoon in the kitchen and get my address book," she said as she untied her apron. Jason picked up the gifts and took them to his room, then met her in the dining room. He sat at the rickety maple table and began to thumb through the address book page by page as she leaned over his shoulder.

"How about the Arnolds?" she asked.

Jason looked at her with a blank expression on his face. "I don't even know who they are, Mom. Who else do we know that lives way out in Eden Prairie?"

"I don't know, dear. Keep looking while I dry the dishes."

After half an hour of intense study, Jason concluded that the only possible prospect was Aunt Hallie Dempsey, but she was over eighty and lived beyond Eden Prairie.

"Hey, Jace," his mother called from the kitchen. "You were in the hospital for six weeks. Could it be someone you met there? A patient? A doctor? One of those nice nurses?"

"I don't know," he said absently. "I just don't know."

His hospital room had been on the second floor of the Ramsey Medical Center. The other bed in the room had been filled only once with a kid so doped up that he never talked to Jason. After three days, the nurses moved the boy to another room, leaving Jason all alone again.

His mother and sisters tried to visit every evening. He remembered how grave and serious Connie and Laura were the first time they saw him with his arms in casts, face and neck covered with bandages, and one leg in traction. Everyone looked at him with such pity. He tried to avoid his mother's eyes the most. He was afraid she knew, afraid she might ask, "Why?"

The hospital personnel and emergency paramedics had referred to the car crash as "an unfortunate accident" and called him "poor kid" once they found out he wasn't drunk.

How could he explain that he had vowed never to drink alcohol as long as he lived? He broke seven ribs and both arms, his pelvis, and his nose while stone sober. He had wanted to die, but he didn't.

As the days went by in the hospital, he stopped worrying that anyone besides his mother would question him at all. No one cared about anything but getting him to eat. At six feet and 120 pounds, he knew he was too skinny, but he didn't care. Nothing mattered to him.

Jason sat hunched over the address book, his fist under his chin. "I don't know who it could be from the hospital. I don't remember anyone or anything all that well."

His mother came to stand behind him and rested her hands on his shoulders. "Hmmm," she said thoughtfully. "You look through the book again. I have to get back to work on this lasagna. If you need anything, let me know. Do you want ice cream for dessert tonight?"

"Sure. Sure, Mom. That's fine." He stared out the window at the bare tree branches in the backyard.

"What kind would you like? Laura and I are going to the store in a while."

"Oh, any kind," he said as he unfolded himself from the dinette chair. "I don't care. Let Laura pick."

The week after Thanksgiving, a steady sun rose two days in a row, warming up the Twin Cities. On the second 50-degree day, Jason found a yellow slip with the mail when he got home from school. The scrawl was just barely legible, but he could make out his name and knew a parcel was on hold for him. He was curious and decided to walk the eight blocks to the neighborhood mail station.

Hands in his Levi pockets, he ambled toward the Rice Street Station wishing he had his Mustang. The car had been the one advantage to living with his father. Jason still remembered the day his father had called him from Donny's Deluxe Motors on University where he sold used cars.

"Jason, I've got a sweet deal here for you, just a sweet deal!" He talked in a high-pitched, fast voice like the dealers on television commercials. "I just took a trade-in, a '66 Mustang with some minor body damage. It needs a cleaning and a wash-up, but you should see it. You could fix this baby up at school in your mechanics class."

"I don't know, Dad. I've only got about a hundred-twenty dollars saved, so I couldn't do it now." His voice was skeptical and guarded.

"That's the sweet deal, m' boy. I picked these wheels off a guy buying a Jeep. I gave him a trade-in of a hundred fifty bucks!" His father's voice rose to a fever pitch as he said, "One hundred 'n' fifty dollars. Can you believe it? What a dipstick. He could've sold it himself for several hundred dollars if he'd cleaned it up. Donny here at the shop will let me have it for three hundred dollars. You can pay me back twenty or thirty bucks a week. Whaddya say, son? A boy needs a car of his own. Hell! I had my first car before I turned sixteen, and you're almost a year older. So, what's it gonna be? Don't let me down now."

Jason knew better than to argue or reason. When his father got caught up in an idea, it was best to go along. Times like these, Jason wanted to trust his father's judgment and join in the excitement, but every time his father surprised him with a special gift or outing, things turned sour. He still had the shiny, gold Raleigh bike his father had given him for his fourteenth birthday just after his mother and sisters had moved out. It hung from the rafters in the garage, back wheel bent, handlebars broken. Scratched paint and dented derailleur were clear evidence of how his father pinned the bicycle against the wall when he drove too far into the garage one night.

Jason sat on the living room floor watching reruns of *The Incredible Hulk* when the door burst open. His father threw his coat at the couch and stalked across the room. He tried to pick Jason up from the floor by the collar of his shirt, but the boy was too heavy. The neck and sleeve tore away, and his father stumbled forward. Jason scrambled back like a crab until he pressed up against the bottom of the reclining chair. He asked, "What's wrong?"

"Your bike, you son of a bitch," he slurred. "You left it in the middle of the garage."

"No, Dad, I parked it against the wall so there'd be plenty of room for you to—"

His father cut him off. "I buy you something most kids would steal for, and you go an' ruin it. Wrecked my fender, too. You don't know how to take care of anything, do ya?" He leaned over almost nose to nose with Jason, his breath smelling of liquor. "Do ya?" he repeated.

"No, I guess not. I guess not," Jason said through gritted teeth.

His father retreated, running his hand through his short hair. Jason wondered how badly broken his bicycle was. He imagined it damaged beyond repair. His father had a habit of destroying things; Jason had a habit of not believing anything would last.

Now he wondered how this car could last, but when his father asked again, "Well? What do you think about the car?"

Jason simply said, "Okay." Let his father set it all up.

Jason had no idea how expensive a car could be. Within three months, he'd bought two steel-belted radials, repaired the clutch and hand brake, replaced the worn seat covers, and bought gallons of gasoline. He liked working on the car. His shop teacher showed him how to repair the dented front fenders and the most serious door dings.

His father was right. It was a good car with a sound engine. It didn't even have a hundred-thousand miles on it yet. Working extra hours after school and on weekends at the New Vista Video shop, he paid his father off in six weeks. The car was his, free and clear.

That was last year. Now he was on foot, and he didn't have a job. As he trudged toward the post office, he felt sad and lost. He looked down and brought his high-top basketball shoe forward, kicking a round rock halfway up the block ahead of him. He could see the roof of the post office further up the street as he passed the apartments by the Coffee Cup Cafe.

He entered the foyer of the postal station and waited in line. The glass windows all around him were frosted white with moisture. When he finally reached the front of the line, he exchanged his yellow slip for a bulky, thick package. Things in it thumped from side to side, back and forth. It wasn't too heavy, but it was awkward, and he wasn't sure whether he should open it on the counter next to the built-in mailboxes or wait until he got home. After a moment's hesitation, he chose to wait and made his way out the door.

When he got home, he took his present to his room and sat on the bed with the package on his knees. He wrested off his jean jacket and tossed it up on the pillow, then ripped the wrapping off the box and lifted the lid.

"Whoa!" he said. A box of 48 Caran d'Arche colored pencils lay next to a package of Schwann-Stabilo fat leads in basic colors. He pulled them out and underneath found a pocket sketchbook, a spiral-bound sketchpad, and a packet of Fabriano artist's paper. He knew the paper was handmade and very expensive, so he was surprised to find thirty sheets each of rough, medium, and smooth surfaced paper.

Jason stood and went to his desk, turned on the light, and sat in the beat-up wooden chair. With eager hands, he ripped the plastic off the pencil boxes, and poured the pencils out on the desk. He pulled a tray out of the desk drawer and began to sort and organize the pencils by color: black, dark blues, light blues, dark forest greens to yellow green, six shades of yellow, flesh, white, light oranges to ocher red, burnt sienna to dark umber brown. Taking a sheet from the Fabriano packet, he began to shade in an area with Tuscan red, and then hatched over it with indigo blue. After experimenting for a short time, he got out his old gray sketchpad and flipped through several pages to one of his recent line drawings. With a light charcoal gray, he began to shade in the fender of a Ford Mustang.

Two hours later, Connie knocked on his door. "Jason, can I come in?"

"Go away," he said, intent on blending several brown and beige colors on the car.

"It's important," she whined.

"Oh, all right."

Connie peeked in as she opened the door, then stepped in and pulled it shut behind her. "Jason," she whispered.

"What?" he answered with irritation in his voice. He did not look up from his drawing.

"Laura's birthday is Saturday, and I don't got any money." She inched toward his desk and leaned over his shoulder to see his project. "That is so cool, Jace! Where did you get all the art stuff?"

"The guardian angel sent it." He stopped for the first time since opening the package and realized he still did not know who the gift-giver was.

"You lucky buck," she said. When he didn't respond, she went on to say, "Remember how we used to make those traveling trip boxes when we were little?"

"You're still little," he said as he continued to draw.

She punched him lightly in the arm. "I am not. I'm almost eleven."

"Hey! You'll mess up my picture. Yeah, I remember the travel boxes." Jason had always enjoyed assembling travel kits for vacations. He began putting them together at age five, boxes of things to do while he rode in the car with his parents. At first, his mother helped him. She bought him stickers, crayons, glue sticks, felt-tip markers, and lots of paper. By the time he was twelve, he began to create sophisticated projects on his own. Using butcher paper, he drew princesses and dragons, knights and kings and castles for Connie to cut out and color when they went on trips. From the thin cardboard in men's shirt packages, he made large paper dolls complete with cutout clothes. He clipped construction paper to create tiny blocks ready to be stacked into houses or whatever in the back seat of the car.

"Jason, let's make Laura an activity box for her birthday. Please, Jason? Will you help me?"

"Hmmm. Okay. You find the perfect box to decorate, and I'll start it out with my old set of colored pencils."

"All right! This'll be great." She danced toward the door, her face all smiles. "It'll be just like old times," she said as she whipped the door open and disappeared into the hall.

Jason leaned back in his chair. *Just like old times,* he thought. *No way. I don't ever want the old times again.*

Weeks passed, punctuated by occasional packages. A leather basketball and a Swiss Army knife—complete with tweezers, bottle opener, scissors, pick, and blades—didn't merit the excitement of the art supplies, but each gift pleased Jason. Still, he found himself puzzling over the identity of the guardian angel.

On the first school day after Christmas vacation, Jason arrived home to find a letter poking out from the mail slot. He pulled at it and heard several other items rustle to the floor inside the house. When he saw his name on the envelope, he brightened for a moment, thinking the gift-giver was finally writing to reveal him or herself. As he reached into the pocket of his coat for his house key, he saw the return address on the back flap: *Stillwater Prison* rubber-stamped in very small letters.

Jason took a step sideways and sagged against the wrought iron railing, his hands clammy, blood pounding in his ears. His head felt as heavy as a bowling ball. He turned, sat on the top step, and stared at the toes of his shoes forcing the scuffmarks to come into focus, crystal clear. Then he ripped open the envelope. The letter read:

> *Dear Jason,*
>
> *Been here three months now, and I guess three months is what I got left if all goes right. It's not so bad, but the holidays were lonely. I miss you and the girls, and I got a lot of things to say to you. I'm in this program here, and my counselor says I need to confront all the ways I went and hurt each person in my life. I'd rather do it in person, but I have no choice and have to write to you.*
>
> *You and me—we started out doing so good until somewhere along the line it was like things just shorted out one wire after another until all I'm left holding is an empty*

fuse box. I don't quite know what to say or do to repair it all. You know I'm sorry. Won't ever happen again.

Family Day here is on January 25th. Would you think about coming up for a visit? Like I say, I got a lot more things to talk over with you.

Love,

Dad

Jason sat on the porch in the cold wind with the envelope in one hand and the letter in the other. He sat motionless until most of his body felt as numb as his mind. He saw a little girl in red snow boots and a yellow coat walk by. She looked at him as she passed, face full of squinting curiosity, and her gait slowed to an even shuffle. Jason stood and turned away, groping in his pocket for his key. He let himself in the house and went to sit in the green chair.

What now? he thought. Tears welled up in his eyes. *What the hell does he want with me now?* He took a deep breath and coughed with force—twice. He felt so cold despite the winter jacket he still wore. He stood and went to adjust the thermostat, turning it up from 62 to 78 degrees. Then he turned and paced from one side of the living room to the other.

The sound of car doors slamming startled Jason from his mindless pacing. His mother and sisters were home. When he heard the key in the door, he grabbed the letter from the coffee table and fled upstairs to his room.

Moments later, he heard his mother calling. "Jason? Jason, honey, we're home." She advanced to the foot of the stairs. "Why do you have the heat up so high?"

He didn't answer. Then he heard her come up the stairs. She knocked on the door. "May I come in?"

"Yeah."

She opened the door and started to speak, but he turned his face and tense shoulders away from her. She shut the door and went to sit in his desk chair facing him as he sat twisted on his twin bed.

"What is it, Jason? What's the matter?" Without a word, he grabbed up the letter and handed it to her. She read it through and didn't say anything. After a minute or two passed, he looked up at her, his eyes wild and flashing.

"I don't want nothin' to do with him. I won't go! He's just lying again. You can't make me go see that son of a bitch!"

"Oh, Jason," she said in a quiet, even tone. "I'm not asking you or telling you to go at all. That's your decision." She stood up and looked around at the walls of his room. Over his bed was a poster-sized drawing of Superman taking off, one knee raised and right fist aimed toward the sky. Above his dresser and radiator were charcoal portraits of a farmyard in a storm, a boat wrecked on a reef, and a deep-sea diver swimming underwater. Around the niche into which his desk fit were sketches of his Mustang, including an unfinished one of a car smashed into a tree.

"Why won't he just leave me alone now, Mom? He makes me feel crazy," Jason said, his voice cracking.

His mother nervously clenched her hands together and looked down at her gray pleated skirt. "Jason, maybe he is finally getting some help. It's hard to know, but maybe he means to do right this time."

"Bullshit! He doesn't give a damn about me! He doesn't care. He just wants me to be there when he gets out so I'll take care of his house, clean up after him, do his laundry." He paused to suck in a breath, "And be there when he needs a punching bag or someone to pick on." His voice was bitter, and he sat on the edge of his bed, twisting the coverlet in both his large hands as if he were strangling it.

They stared at one another for a moment before his mother said in a faint voice, "I wanted to come get you long ago, son. But sometimes he hit me, and at first he made threats about taking the girls away. They were too little to defend themselves, and you always seemed to be able to defuse most of his anger. I knew he was rough on you, but I, well, I . . ." Her voice broke. She struggled to stay calm. Clearing her throat and swallowing, she met his eyes and said, "I let you stay there because you kept telling me everything was all right."

Jason looked away. He closed his eyes tightly and said, "I don't know why I kept saying that. I don't know. He was nicest to me the summer after you left. He was so—lost. And he was fine when he wasn't drinking. It just kept getting worse, little by little, and I couldn't make him stop. Honest, I couldn't."

"You don't have to go back to him ever now. I wish you had told him you wanted to come live here. I think he might have let you. Why didn't you say something?"

"Oh, Mom, what do you mean?" he cried in anguish. "You left me there with him. You knew what he was like, and still you left me there." He bounced up off the bed and went to stand at the window with his back to her. "Besides, somebody had to take care of him."

She turned in the chair and said, "Jason, please. Look at me. This is important." He glanced over his left shoulder, body still half turned to the window. "Son, you don't have to take care of him ever again. That's not your job. You have enough to do to take care of yourself. Sons don't look after their parents; parents look after their sons."

His fists clenched and his eyes blazed with fury as he turned to face her. "Then where were *you*? Where were you when I needed someone to take care of me? Why didn't you come get me? Where in the hell were you?" His face crumpled as he fought back tears. Stumbling over to the bed, he flopped face down with his head cradled in his hands and cried.

Jason felt his mother's eyes upon him. He tried to calm himself, but he felt embarrassed. Abruptly his mother stood, took two tissues from the box on his bedside table and tucked them into his hand. He sat up and blew his nose, and she sat next to him on the bed. She put her arm across his hunched shoulders and patted him with awkward care.

"I did it on purpose, Mom. I'm really sorry now, but I did it on purpose." His whisper was a hoarse rasp.

"Did what?"

"Ran into that tree. It was all my fault. I—"

"I know."

"—meant to—what?" He looked up at her. "What did you say?"

"I said, I know, Jason. I figured that out."

He gazed at her in amazement, his mouth gaping open. "How?"

"I just did. I put two and two together from how you acted in the hospital and from what the police said about arresting your father."

"Then why didn't you say something?"

His mother stepped away and went to lean against the window frame. She looked down at her hands, rubbing them as if they were cold. "I tried to talk to you in the hospital, Jason, but you were so depressed. We've needed to have this conversation, but I couldn't get through to you. You obviously didn't want to talk to anybody, and I didn't know what to do." She stood and went to sit in the desk chair. "So, tell me now. What happened? What really happened?"

Jason didn't know how to explain, and he didn't want to talk about it or think about it. He couldn't keep the images from coming to him, though.

Things had occurred in such a blur. He came home from his job at the video store late one Saturday night and found his father sitting on the sofa with the usual can of beer in his hand.

"You borrowed my car," his father snarled, "and it sure drives like hell now. You been hot-roddin' in it too much. Fenders are all out of line."

"What?" Jason had waxed the car only last weekend, and the Gran Torino should still be in excellent condition. He opened the screen door and squinted into the darkness. He couldn't see the front of the car, so he walked out in the warm night air to the driveway. The right headlight was broken, the fender dented in, and the grill looked odd. He reached down to touch a strange splotch on the hood and drew back a hand coated with sticky oil or mud. As he turned back to the house, the light from the front window shone upon him, and he realized blood covered his hand.

Panicked, he rushed into the house and faced his father. "Dad! This is blood. You hit a deer or something, right?"

His father took a swig of his beer, then tipped his head back, eyelids drooping, and stared at his son. Jason stepped closer and held his hand up, five fingers spread.

"What happened, Dad? What the hell happened?"

In a menacing voice, his father said, "Don't you swear at me." He smacked the can down on the side table, leaving a scratch, and sat forward. With effort, he lurched to his feet. As he advanced, Jason stepped back holding up his bloody hands.

"So you hit somebody," he slurred. "You lil' son of a bitch." He staggered, but he managed to grab Jason's tee shirt.

"No, Dad. No!" His hands came up to grip his father's arms, leaving a handprint of blood on the tattered sweatshirt sleeve. His father pushed him back against the wall.

"Oh yeah. Anybody comes looking—you did it. I got buddies— buddies who'll back me up—say I was at the other pub. I was, you know." He leaned into Jason and chuckled.

"Dad! Dad, we gotta call the police." He pulled away from his father's grip and reached for the phone on the end table. His father stopped laughing and gave Jason a mighty shove, sending him sprawling onto the davenport.

"You touch that phone again, and I'll rip your goddamn head off! I got three DWIs. This one puts me behind bars. You tell 'em you did it, or I'll kick the shit outta you!" He grabbed his son's arm again with both hands and dragged him to his feet.

Despite his whole upper body shaking, Jason managed a calm, level voice. "No, Dad. I won't." His father curled up his left fist, but slapped Jason with his right hand instead. In a panic, Jason threw his arms up to protect his face, but his father punched him in the stomach.

When he doubled over, his father grabbed the neck of his shirt, but Jason managed to twist away. He lurched across the room and escaped into the night. Behind him, he heard his father shouting, "You did it, you sonuvabitch. I'll tell 'em you did it, and they'll come get you. Go ahead and run—they'll get you . . ."

Jason turned to run, but he couldn't breathe. He made great gasping sounds as he dug the car keys out of his pocket. He leaned up against the Mustang, took a big breath, and eased himself behind the wheel. Pulling away from the curb, he gunned down the avenue, shifting into third and careening around the corner, tires squealing.

They won't get me, he thought. And he'll never get me again, either. He won't get me. He won't. I'm getting away forever.

The Mustang roared along the upward incline of the county road, bouncing over the crest of the hill. He saw the old elm tree off to the right at the bottom. With a reckless surge of energy, he put the accelerator to the floor. The car left the pavement, skidding in the soft shoulder of gravel toward the elm before he realized what he was doing. He slammed on the brakes, but it was too late. He didn't even have time to raise his hands to protect himself before the car struck the tree head-on. The last sensation he remembered was cool air on his face as he flew from the car, hit something hard, and lost consciousness.

Jason sat on the bed in his room, looking down at the floor. "Mom, I can't explain it so it makes sense. Sometimes I think back to that night, and I almost can't believe it happened. Dad hit the guy, came home, and tried to blame it on me. When I wanted to call the police, he started beating on me, and I just couldn't take it anymore." In a whisper, he said, "I couldn't live like that anymore. I just—wanted—well, I wanted to die. That's about it."

His mother sat quietly, listening to Jason. Her eyes came to rest upon a small drawing above the light switch by the door. A black planet spun around, encircled by colorful rings of motion. Little red explosions blasted all around the planet. The sketch was mounted on a white piece of construction paper.

She turned to Jason and looked at his pallid face. His eyes seemed peaceful, though his nose was red and he sniffled. He leaned forward, elbows on knees, and rested his face on his fists.

"I'm so sorry you didn't come to me, Jason. Three people saw your father hit the pedestrian when he blasted out of the lot at Smokey Joe's. It's lucky he didn't kill the man. It's even luckier he didn't kill you."

They sat in silence.

"As long as we are confessing things, Jason, I need to tell you about the guardian angel gifts."

He snapped to attention. With his eyes narrowing, a slight smile appeared on his face. "You," he said. "*You* sent the packages." It was a statement, not a question. "Why, Mom? How come you faked me out the way you did?"

"I was afraid for you. I couldn't seem to get through to you. I figured that if you really did run into that tree on purpose, you might try to hurt yourself again. But you wouldn't talk about it. So, one day, I bought you a wooden box and decided on impulse to fill it with candy and bring it home to you. Then it occurred to me to send it by mail, and I asked one of my co-workers who lives in Eden Prairie to drop it off for me when he went to the post office on the way home from work. I meant to tell you at first, but then I waited." She looked down and shook her head, then went on. "Jason, I wanted you to know you were loved, that someone cared. I sent that little note and tried to imagine myself about eighty-five-years old so you wouldn't guess who was sending things." She chuckled. "But after the note and the chain arrived, I definitely didn't know what to do. You didn't talk for days—just wandered around like you were in a trance."

She got up and walked to the window. Jason saw drifts of snow with little whirls of light snow dust blowing up and around the pane. "I started to get frantic," she said. "I sent things as fast as I could think of them or afford them, and slowly, you seemed to come around."

She turned to face her son. He gazed at her in silence. Suddenly he blurted out, "Promise me you won't make me go live with him ever again!"

"Don't worry. I won't let him hurt you anymore."

"I'm more worried about me hurting him." His voice held a fierce edge. "Sometimes I just want to kill him."

"Jason!"

"It's true, Mom. He makes me so mad. I'm afraid I'll lose control the same way he does—you know—like father, like son."

"No, that's not the way it works. He's got a drinking problem, and he's more immature than you are. You're not like him at all."

He leaned back on the bed and relaxed.

"Guess I better get some supper going now," his mother said as she moved toward the door.

"Mom?"

"Yes, dear?"

"If you think I should, I'll go see Dad and have it out with him."

She stopped short and turned to gape at her son. "I thought you said you never wanted to see him again."

"Sometimes I do, and sometimes I don't. Sometimes . . ." He fumbled for words. "Sometimes I still worry about him." His eyes were downcast, and he looked as though he might cry again.

"Jason, let's give this a lot of time. We should probably get a counselor and work it out when you are ready. Don't worry about it just yet. All right?"

He nodded. "Okay. Thanks, Mom."

She opened the door and left the room. Jason sat for a few moments, his mind racing, then stood up and stretched. He went to sit at his desk, turned on the desk lamp, and opened his sketchpad. Flipping to a blank page, he picked up a grass green pencil and began to draw.

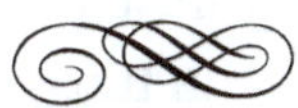

Strange Inclinations

My parents can't understand the way I have changed. Actually, I haven't changed at all. I've just become who I always was, but had hidden all those years. "Linnae, we never knew you had these strange and unusual inclinations," they keep saying. "What did we do wrong?"

They're appalled that I have taken up with Sharon. That's what they say: *taken up with.* They can't understand why she and I are together instead of me and their soon-to-be-ex son-in-law.

They're aghast about my choices and think I need psychiatric evaluation. Most of all, they can't fathom why I split with Scotty. "But we thought you were happy."

Happy? They thought I was happy? What they didn't know could have killed me.

I made my decision to leave my husband while submerged with my back flat against the smooth porcelain tub. All I did was walk down the hallway, past the open bathroom door, and the next thing I knew, I was lifted off my feet and flying through space. I still have the clearest vision of translucent bubbles swirling around my face and my eyes burning. Everything sounded muffled. I opened my mouth to scream, but shut it quickly when water poured in and made me choke. My lungs burned. I felt the weight of his fists, grasping my sweatshirt and pressing against my collarbone and stomach. I kicked. I pushed. I waved and flailed and punched—all to no avail. He has always been so very much stronger than I am.

In a flash, I knew he would kill me—was killing me. *Oh God, I* thought, *please! Get me out of here, and I swear, this time I'll go. I'll pack up the baby and flee. I will. I will. I promise. Oh God, I promise!*

Just then, Scotty's hold loosened, and I reached for the sides of the tub and pulled with all my might. My head popped out of the water, and I gasped in air.

"Bitch!" he screamed. "I should kill you! Where's the money?" He pushed my head back under, but he was unsteady from all the effort and the effect of the alcohol he'd drunk. I curled to my side and strained to swing my feet around so that in an instant, I was wedged sideways in the tub, my face out of the water, feet pressing against one side and one arm slung over the wet porcelain, my head barely clear of the water. I held on like a hermit crab in his shell.

Scotty sat back on the floor, wheezing and spent. I stood and water rushed off me. My jeans hung heavy and loose. I looked down at the water in the bathtub. It was amazing to me that I could have drowned in only four inches of water. Gallons of water had splashed on the floor and were probably dripping through the floorboards to further warp the linoleum in the kitchen below. I didn't care. I stepped out of the tub and resisted the urge to kick Scotty, knowing it would only provoke him. I left the bathroom, and there, leaning against the wall outside the door in his too tight toddler-sized pajamas, stood my son. Tears stained his face, and his eyes were blank. "Kyle," I said. "Kyle, honey." He didn't respond, as though he couldn't hear me.

I picked him up under the arms and he hung in the air like a sack of potatoes, which was probably okay since if he'd grabbed onto me, I'd have soaked him. I carried him into the bedroom and settled him on the double bed. I locked the door and changed into a nightgown, leaving the wet clothes in a pile on top of my soaked shoes. Then I lay down on the bed and pulled Kyle to me. His body felt cool and damp. I covered us up with the spread and hummed a lullaby.

Gradually, he warmed and began to squirm. He reached up with tiny fingers and grabbed a lock of my wet hair and wrapped it around his hand. His other hand went into his mouth, and his eyes closed. He slept.

I didn't leave that night. I knew I had at least two weeks before Scotty's next drunken rampage. He generally got this way the day before payday when we had no money left for booze or pot. Though I knew I had made a promise, I figured God would allow me a short period of time to get organized. After Scotty went to work each morning, I sat in the kitchen of our ugly cracker-box house and made lists of everything Kyle and I would need to set up housekeeping elsewhere. I had limited space, so I resolved to be strategic.

A few days before the next payday, I packed up everything of value that Kyle and I owned: most of my clothes, the grocery money, my jewelry, my collection of tiny crystal figurines, and the savings bonds I had bought when I was still working, which Scotty had—thankfully—forgotten about. I packed all of Kyle's clothes, diapers, and toys into three duffel bags and dismantled his little bed so I could cram it into the back of the station wagon. I fit the high chair in the back seat, but the collapsible playpen was too wide, so I left it behind. Kyle wouldn't need it anyway.

I went through the entire house, room by room, and stuffed into brown paper grocery bags everything that I could: dish towels, pots and pans, spices, dry food items, canned goods, cups and mugs, the toaster, dishes, Tupperware containers, cleaning supplies, toilet paper, bath towels and washcloths, the first aid kit, soap, shampoo, and the entire drawer of stuff in the bathroom. I didn't have time to pack as tight as I could have because I didn't know whether Scotty would go directly to the bar after work or stop by home first.

I was nearly done in the bathroom when I heard a noise at the back door. A flash of panic ripped through me. *How could he be home so soon? Oh, my God, help me!* Everywhere I looked, the house was a mess. *He'll know. He'll know.* I shivered with a chill that gripped me through and through.

A soft voice called out, "Hel-loooo."

For a moment, I thought my legs might give out. *Judy. It's only Judy.*

I stepped out of the bathroom and greeted my neighbor at the back door.

"I thought you were home, I knocked, but . . ."

The look on my face must have given it all away.

"Linnae," she said as she stepped inside, glancing about the room at the bags on the floor and all over the counters. "What's going on?"

"Judy, you can't tell. Promise me you won't tell."

"Tell what?"

"I'm leaving. And if you tell him anything—well, let's just say, it won't be pretty."

She pressed her lips together and looked out the kitchen window. She didn't speak for a moment, and I didn't know what to say. An uncomfortable silence hung in the room, and all I cared to know was whether she would rat me out or keep this to herself. When she met my eyes, she said, "I should have said something, done something." She stared down at her shoes. "I knew," she whispered. "I just didn't know what to say. I'm sorry."

I didn't expect that from her, and the regret in her voice brought tears to my eyes. "It's not like you could have done anything."

"But I wish I had. Is there anything I can do to help now?"

"Yes. You can keep my secret—pretend you never saw me leave."

She nodded. "That I can and will do."

So I let her help me carry things out to the station wagon, and she did a great job packing things in—much better than I could do in my apprehensive state.

I wrote a final note:

> *Scotty, It's over. You'll be getting divorce papers in the mail.*
> *DO NOT come after Kyle and me. I absolutely will not come*
> *back. If you come after me, I WILL tell. It's over, and that's it.*
> *~Linnae*

I took my slumbering son from where he lay on the couch and carried him out to the car. Judy hugged me goodbye, and Kyle and I drove away.

We never looked back.

I now realize I have always been attracted to women. When I was six, I had a babysitter named Gina, a slim, dark-haired teenager of sixteen. I just loved her. Literally. I always wanted to sit right next to her on the couch, or lay all over her if I could, while we ate popcorn and watched TV when my parents were out. I refused to go to bed on time and insisted I sleep wrapped in a blanket on the couch next to her. When my parents came home, they shook me awake, scolded me for disobeying, and ran me off to my room. It didn't stop me from doing the same thing again whenever Gina came over.

I was in heaven when Gina babysat me—at least until she started bringing her big lummox of a boyfriend with her. I was relegated to her feet or to the rocker or lounge chair. I couldn't bear it. I had this image in my mind of Gina and me spending the rest of our lives sitting on the sofa, me holding her hand, and watching TV movies.

Instead, Dean—with the ugly, shaved head and tight jeans—was the one carrying out my fantasy. I was heartbroken and demanded that my parents get me a new babysitter, which they did: Mona Peysen, a morose and soft-spoken seventeen-year-old from the next block. She never brought any boyfriends over, but it never mattered. She didn't have that spark Gina had. When it came time to go to bed, I went without a fuss and by flashlight read a book called *Frightening Fairy Tales*.

So you see, I knew my true inclinations in first grade—but I obviously knew society's true attitudes, too, because I exiled my thoughts and feelings for three decades. When I look back at my life, I can recite a list of women with whom I have been smitten over the years, but I kept it a secret—even from myself.

I don't know why I never explained the abuse to my parents, but I always had the feeling they wouldn't believe me. Scotty was always so sweet and polite around them. They have no frame of reference for him as a madman, kicking over our furniture, waving around his .38 handgun, slapping and striking and screaming about everything. In private, he was sullen and angry when he was sober, but he was a wild man when he was drunk. And he liked to drink. No way I could get him to quit or go to treatment or even ease up. He's just like his father—only his father got into a drunk driving accident at Scotty's age and ended up paralyzed in the legs. At least my mother-in-law didn't have to run and hide and protect the kids from him; he couldn't reach them most of the time from the recliner.

I don't know why I married him. Well, yes, I guess I do know. I was thirty-three years old, and it was the thing to do. And he asked. I wasn't brave enough at the time to say no, move to the Cities, and find a woman to love and live with. I bowed to the pressure. Who wouldn't? I feel the power of it even now, and I felt the weight of it chasing me down the freeway the day I fled from the house. I knew he wouldn't let me go, and I knew I had only $230 cash and $800 worth of savings bonds to get to wherever my destination was.

I couldn't call my parents for help. That would be the first place Scotty would look. I did call and leave a message on their machine to tell them I was fine, that I'd left him, and that I'd be in touch. I said I was driving out of state to stay with an old high school friend which was not true. Instead, I drove to the Twin Cities, carried my sleeping two-year-old into the phone booth with me, looked at the yellow pages, and called an emergency help line. They sent me to a battered women's shelter, and in a matter of days, I completed an array of paperwork to get welfare, food stamps, and temporary housing. All I needed was a few weeks, tops. I knew I could get a secretarial job—even through a temp agency—if I had some time. They told me legal action would be taken to get child support from Scotty. He'd know what county we lived in. I didn't know if they had already contacted him or if they would in the future, so I rushed and found work with a small firm in a suburb.

The Hennepin County worker was surprised when I came in and closed out all the welfare. I told her they could deep-six the child support paperwork, and she said not to worry, that it would take three months just to process the general papers and longer to do the legal part. If I had known that, I would have been a lot less panic-stricken, but who cares? I had a job, and I was ready to use the savings bonds to rent an apartment.

Kyle and I were safe. Finally safe.

It's been two years since I left him. I hear he's taken up with a new woman, and all I can say is that my prayers are with her. I met Sharon last year while I was volunteering at a battered women's shelter. Miranda, her little girl, is four, and she and Kyle took to one other right away. Miranda said she'd always wanted a little brother, so she was ecstatic when Sharon and I merged households. I was thrilled, too. I swear, what I put myself through before I finally let myself live.

My grandmother used to have a sign in her kitchen written in Norwegian. Translated, it said something like: *We get too soon old and too late smart.* Isn't that the truth? It took me most of my life to reconcile my "strange inclinations," but I have. I no longer care what others think, and I don't care if my parents ever understand. They think I'm unhappy, that anyone with my deviant lifestyle—that's what they call it—would be unhappy. But I'm not. For the first time in my life, I'm finally safe, happy, and strangely inclined to stay that way.

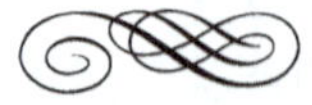

Jumping Over My Head

High jump is a tricky athletic event. The object is to "beat the bar." The bar is a lightweight, black-and-white pole, which is fifteen feet long with a diameter of one-inch. Flattened at both ends, it rests securely on top of two adjustable vertical posts and can be raised up by inches on the posts. After jumping to clear the bar—or knocking it off the posts— the jumper falls into a cushy pit made of compacted foam rubber.

Nowadays, high jump pits are huge and expensive cushions for sky-flying athletes, but the first jump pits I encountered in grade school were piles of sawdust. Fortunately, few sixth graders ever jumped much over three-and-a-half feet. Back then, I used the scissors approach and ran up to the bar, planted my left foot and leapt, kicking my right foot out straightaway from my body and as high as I could. At the peak of the jump, when I had gotten my hips as high in the air as possible, I'd kick up my left leg while my right leg started downward on the other side of the bar, hence the scissors effect. It worked great because I was able to land on my feet. The only complication occurred when some unlucky kid got one foot over the bar, failed to clear it, and then straddled the bar and fell on it. I didn't like being that unlucky kid and was very careful.

Before she abandoned me, my mother used to holler, "Quit bouncing around! You can't high jump here on the couch." I was crushed because I wanted to show her what I'd learned.

Seems like the most frequent words out of my mouth were "Watch me!" I wanted someone to take notice, someone who mattered. It seemed I could never put on a good enough spectacle or one exciting enough to get the attention I needed: high jumping wasn't as thrilling to people as the hundred-yard dash or the pole vault. But it was what I was good at. So until I met my best friend Katie during sophomore year, most of the time I was a lonely competitor, far away from the excitement of the oval, marking my steps, gauging the wind, sharpening my spikes, and trying to get an extra inch of lift to help me avoid landing on the bar.

No girl in the history of my high school has ever jumped as high as I did, and I suspect none has ever jumped so high while feeling so low. I was tied up in knots of confusion about Katie, about my feelings, about everything in my life. Only action and movement, the constant release of kinetic energy, could assuage the puzzle I was to myself.

I don't remember how I met Katie, which seems odd since I can remember whole conversations we later had and entire trips we took to William O'Brien State Park with my foster family. The one truth about which I am dead sure—now—is that I loved her more than anyone else in my young life, with the exception of perhaps my mother. But you don't choose to love your mother; it's a natural fact of life. A best friend, on the other hand, is supposed to be a platonic relationship. I knew that and pressed back all knowledge of my feelings for her, speaking in code to myself, writing casual and smart-aleck notes in class, aching for every moment I was able to spend with her.

Katie taught me there was comfort and security in love, and she made me believe I was lovable. She did this by paying attention to me, by listening, and by opening a tiny crack in the sealed vault that was my heart.

Intuition told me not to talk about my feelings—not to her, not to anyone. So, carefree and wisecracking, I covered up my intense longing to express my love. It wasn't safe, and I was too afraid.

The summer after our sophomore year, my foster parents planned to take off to a lake for two weeks of water skiing, inner-tubing, and lying in the sun. Katie's parents said she could go, and I was so happy I didn't care who knew it. I remember the vacation as sun-dappled and warm. I have two photographs from then. One shows Katie leaning up against the boat, squinting into the sun, her face and shoulders tan and smooth. She is thin and pensive, a girl-child already shying away from the camera. The other photo is of me skiing behind the speedboat, far away at the end of a fifty-foot rope. I cannot see my face, but I can make out my sky-blue two-piece swimsuit and the muscles straining in my thighs. I have no pictures of us together.

Autumn of my junior year in high school I met Mark Collins, one of the new assistant track and field coaches. A big, hearty-looking blond with a wind-burnt face, Coach Collins was a high jump specialist. He had been a college champion using the straddle method. He showed me how he used a fast, running approach from the left of the foam rubber pit. As he neared the metal bar, he transformed his forward motion upward by planting his left foot hard, swinging his right knee up and across his chest, and rotating his body to the left. His right knee and arm slipped over the bar first, followed by the left half of his body as he wormed his way over, face downward, without touching the bar, and landed triumphantly in the foam pit.

By the time I met Coach Collins, I'd graduated from the scissors technique to the Flop, made famous at the 1972 Olympics by the American champion Dick Fosbury. After measuring a right angle to the pit and running the tape thirty-two feet out, I'd mark the route with white adhesive tape. The Flop required me to make a speedy semi-circular run toward the bar until my right shoulder was less than three feet from it. Then I planted my left foot as hard as I could and kicked my right knee up and to the left as I threw my arms high in the air. I leaned back, going over the bar headfirst and backwards. At the height of the jump, I arched my back as though I were a hissing cat, and then piked into a sitting position and tried to kick my feet up and away from the bar. In a successful jump, I powered up and slithered over the bar using my center of gravity perfectly. A poorly timed jump resulted in

                    L o r i   L.   L a k e

my neck, back or legs landing on the metal bar, which made for some interesting bruises.

Coach Collins solved some of the bruise problems. After watching me progress to heights near five feet, he saw that I became hesitant and often shied away. "Chris, how do I talk you into believing you can clear the bar?" he asked me.

I shrugged, and he walked away with a puzzled look on his face.

The next day he showed up at practice with a three-foot-square wooden springboard. "Try this out," he said. "Got it from the gymnastics coach."

I jumped on it and launched up and out at least two feet higher than I expected and came down so hard on the tar track that it hurt the balls of my feet.

Coach Collins dragged the springboard near the pit and placed it over my take-off mark. He took down the black-and-white bar and tossed it in the grass beside the pit. "Okay, Chris. Go ahead and make your approach. Plant here on the board, and go through your jump like the bar was there."

I did what he told me, and as I planted my foot and launched up into the air, I found myself soaring higher than I ever had. Startled, I came down into the pit hard on my shoulders with the rest of my body following. The foam cushioned my fall. "Wow!" I said. "I like that."

I did a few more practice tries, and then he put the bar back up at the five-foot level. "Now, use the best form you can, and concentrate on arching and piking, not on powering up."

I cleared five feet with lots of room to spare and filled up with excitement. After each jump, Coach moved the posts up another inch, and soon I had jumped five feet eight inches. When he moved it up to five foot nine, I got set, started off on my approach, but then shied away at the last moment. Hands on his hips, he gave me a quizzical look.

"Coach," I said, "it's over my head."

"So?"

"Well, I can't even *see* over it—how am I supposed to clear it? Besides, I doubt I'll get anywhere near it later without a springboard. What good does it do?"

"Faith, Chris. You need a little faith. What's your highest jump so far—without this board, I mean?"

"Five two," I answered.

"That's nothing compared to what you can do," he said in an excited voice, as he strolled up to me. "If you can imagine yourself— feel and see yourself—clearing that height, then you can do it. I've watched you. Your center of gravity, here," his index fingers poked at my hipbones, "needs only to get higher than the bar. The rest is all technique in arching and piking. How tall are you?"

"A shade under five-seven."

"How high is your vertical jump?"

"Oh, thirty-two inches, maybe thirty-three."

"Chris, if you add thirty-three inches to the forty inches extending from the ground to your center of gravity, how many feet is that?" He had a mischievous smile on his face.

"Over six feet."

"Right. Giving yourself a couple inches leeway, there's no reason why you can't jump five-nine, five-ten—or *more* this year. And if you increase your vertical jump and improve your technique, you'll go higher. When you get home tonight, get a piece of string and tack it six feet high from one side of your bedroom to the other. Every time you walk in the room, visualize yourself jumping up and over it." He knocked on his forehead and said, "It's all in your head, Chris. If you believe you can do it, if you *imagine* yourself doing it, you will. Think about it."

I thought about it a lot. I strung a piece of red yarn up in my tiny bedroom, and I kept thinking about jumping over my head. Katie came to my track meets and sat along the edge of the high jump apron to cheer me on. My jumps began inching up over five feet on a regular basis. Soon I was managing five-three consistently, and then I hit five-four, which qualified me for the state championship. I couldn't believe my good luck. I was only a junior in high school, and I was going to the state meet in two months.

Katie took me out for pizza that night, and she couldn't stop hugging me. "I'm so proud of you," she said.

Spring is a time of flowers budding, the sun coming up early and setting late, a time of growth and newfound love. Sitting on a dock, dragging our feet in the cold lake water one day in late April, Katie asked me if I planned to go on to college.

"Hope so, but it all depends on getting a scholarship. Did you get the results from your junior aptitude test?"

"Nope."

"Me neither, but I hope I did okay. They don't give much to girls for track scholarships. I'd like to go to one of the local colleges."

"Not me," Katie said. "I want to get as far away from my folks as I can."

I felt a moment of alarm. "But Katie, if we both went somewhere around here, we could room together." I hadn't thought this out very well, but as soon as I said it, I knew it was a great idea.

She put her arm across my shoulder, leaned her head against me and sighed. "I don't know. I just don't know what I want. I'm not good at anything like you are. Just my luck, I'll probably get pregnant and my dad will force a shotgun wedding."

"What? You're not—"

"No! No," she said as she laughed. "Sometimes you're such an innocent. Listen, I was just thinking out loud. Tell you what, let's make a pact to see if we can make it to graduation without losing our virginity to one of those stupid, groping boys."

For me it was an instant deal, no hesitation, no second thoughts. I was saving myself for Katie, anyway. I knew it wouldn't be a hard promise to keep.

But later that spring, before the state track meet, she broke the pact.

One night when I stayed over at her house, she casually told me about sleeping with her new boyfriend. I wanted to cry. She tried to put her arms around me and kept asking what was wrong, but I couldn't tell her.

"We'll still be close, maybe not as close as we were, but it'll be okay. This is better," she said as she stroked my cheek.

If it hadn't been so late, I would have walked the eight miles home.

Overnight, everything changed. She couldn't face me the next morning. I gathered up my clothes and took the two records I had loaned her and left. I skipped school the next day, calling in to the school secretary to say in a disguised voice: "Chris is sick with a cold. She'll be in tomorrow."

When I was eleven, I had lost my mother to mental illness. The hospital she lived in was too far away to visit more than once a year. Then when I was twelve, I lost my father when he moved across the country, never writing or calling, rarely visiting. At seventeen, I lost Katie to fear. I couldn't speak up and tell her I wanted to grow up and live with her, to come home from my job each day, eat supper with her, sleep with her, go on vacations together, support one another, and wake up each new day with her face near mine.

Too many losses, and she was the last one before I abandoned my child-like wonder about the magic of love. Now I would be a fortress and seal up my heart so no one could hurt me again. I understood my error. No matter how I felt, I couldn't love Katie; I was the wrong gender.

A confusing spring followed, full of bad dreams and headaches. I avoided Katie at school and spent the next six weeks in a tangle like the knots in the embroidery I gave up in fifth grade. Only one thing kept me going: jumping. That was the one place where I was skilled at avoiding pain. I rarely landed on the bar, never hurt myself badly, and took only carefully calculated risks.

At the state track meet in late May, there were hundreds of kids from all around the state. Only two other athletes from my high school had qualified—two boys: a quarter-miler and a javelin thrower.

The first day of the weekend meet, I only needed to clear five-four to stay in the competition, and we started at five feet. No problem. I was surprised, though, when half the entrants fouled up and were out of the meet within the hour. The rest of us qualified for the finals. Day One of the competition was over.

That evening, Coach Collins and I celebrated over root beer and pizza. I sat with him in the red leather booth at The Pizza Caboose and wished he were my father.

The next morning dawned foggy and damp. The officials broomed water off the rubberized high jump approach as I ran several laps around the track. I stretched my muscles well and did a series of grass drills to loosen up. Other contestants attempted practice jumps, but I could see the jumping plane was slick with moisture. I watched the others warming up and slipping on the special rubberized surface, but I also saw the sun struggling to come out from behind the clouds. I took a few runs to the bar, but despite the quarter-inch spikes on the balls of my track shoes, my spikeless heels skidded enough to throw me off, so I didn't attempt to jump.

The official standing near the jump pit blew a short toot on a whistle and shouted, "Five-minute warning."

I looked back toward the stands and searched for my coach. He stood, and his blond hair waved in the wind like a wheat-colored flag. He held up his hand and shook his head, and I understood: "Don't jump. Not yet."

I nodded, and he made swinging motions with his arms and gestured toward the grassy area in the center of the track.

He wants me to warm up doing grass drills. I ran a slow semi-circle, planted my foot in the loose green grass, and used my arms to power myself upwards. I liked to lean back enough that I felt off balance, and then I piked forward so I landed on my feet and not on my behind. I glanced up at him in the stands. He nodded, then sat down. I did six more careful drills, using the half of the field not occupied by the shot-putters.

"Good morning," the PA announcer echoed into a scratchy microphone. "We start with the first event of the day, the finals for the girls' high jump competition, which will now begin at the opening height of five feet. Shortly, the hundred-meter dashes will begin."

There were twenty-eight jumpers, and I was slated to jump seventh. I stayed close to the jump area so I'd hear my name called. Watching the first six jumpers brought a knot to my stomach. All of them slipped or hesitated near the bar and missed their first jumps. The dampness on the slick surface hadn't dried any. I caught my breath and felt pressure in my neck as I turned to look at Coach Collins in the stands. He was on his feet, waving, trying to catch my attention. He mouthed something, but I couldn't quite make it out. Then he drew his finger across his neck and shook his head.

"Chris Wilson," the jump official called out.

I turned toward the jump apron. I didn't even have my warm-up pants or sweats off. I knew I wasn't ready. I looked back at Coach who was still waving and shouting.

It came to me. *Pass.* He wanted me to pass.

"Pass, sir," I said to the jump official.

He and most of the jumpers turned to stare at me. "Pass?" he said. "You don't get another chance at this, young lady."

"Yes, sir, I know." He turned away and called the next name.

The remaining jumpers took their first attempts at five feet, half of them missing. Only one other competitor, dressed in red warm-ups, passed as I had.

As the official moved the posts and bar up a notch, the PA announcer said, "The bar in the girls' high jump is now being raised two inches to five feet two inches."

The approach still looked slick, and I wasn't sure whether to try it or not. I looked back to Coach, and he shrugged his shoulders. It was up to me. I walked across the grass to the edge of the apron and bent down to feel the rubberized surface. It wasn't dry across the entire apron, though patches were evaporating and no longer looked as slippery.

"Chris Wilson."

I shook my head at the official, knowing it was a gamble, and said, "Pass again." He shook his head in disbelief and called the next name.

The sun popped up over the top of the grandstand and began to beat down on my back. Heat flowed through the warm-up pants and sweatshirt I was wearing. I went back to my grass drills and kept stretching my calves and thighs and Achilles tendons.

Over the next twenty minutes, the jumpers who failed to clear five-two on their first try made their second attempts. I took off my sweat top and bottoms and ran some wind sprints. Other jumpers joined me on the grass to stretch and warm up. Before ten minutes passed, six competitors were disqualified when they missed their third and final attempts at five-foot-two. These were six good jumpers, most of whom had jumped against me during the year, and they were out of the competition at heights most of them scaled with little effort during the regular season.

"In girls' high jump," the announcer said over the booming PA, "the height is now five feet four inches, with one-inch increments hereafter."

By now, the sun burned strong and hot. Tendrils of steam rose from the running track surrounding us. The high jump apron was almost dry. I could see only two shallow puddles of water at the left edge, far from my approach. I looked back to Coach. He stood, laced his fingers together, and shook them over his head in his best prizefighter imitation.

Because the first six jumpers were out, I was now first and was ready each time they called my name at five-four, five-five, and five-six. Each successful jump filled me with exhilaration. After clearing five-feet-six inches, only four of us remained. When I cleared five-seven—for the first time in my life—I somersaulted out of the pit and did a handspring in the grass.

Five-eight was mine, too, but when I piked on the way over, my heel nipped the bar and brought it down into the pit. The bar fell across my hip bones, and I heard an "ahhh" from the spectators in the stadium. For the first time, I realized many people were watching—and watching closely. I rolled out of the pit and looked up at Coach Collins, who raised his fist above his head into the air. "You can do it," his punching fist seemed to say.

To the cheers of the spectators, the red-clad jumper narrowly cleared five-eight, but the other two missed, leaving me with my second try. I checked my steps as I made a practice run past the bar, then I queued up for the approach. I could feel the hum of adrenaline racing through my body, and after several deep breaths, I took off, planted hard, and exploded upward. I arched my back 'til I felt doubled over backward, then piked and kicked my feet up so high my knees bumped me in the chin on the follow-through. As I sank down into the damp foam pit, I squinted up at the bar on the posts, sitting solid and unmoving. I heard the roar of the crowd and crawled out of the pit triumphant.

Five-eight, I thought. Over my head. I'm jumping over my head. Incredible!

Eliza and I both cleared five-nine, but the other two jumpers missed their second and third attempts, leaving only the red-clad girl and me.

"Five-ten," said the voice on the PA, "and we are down to two contestants, Chris Wilson from Stokes High, and Eliza Schmidt from Spartan."

At this point, Eliza and I had matched one another jump for jump except at five-eight, which took her one jump and me two jumps. She was ahead, unless she missed at five-ten, and I managed to clear it on the first try. Five-ten. Over my head. Seriously over my head. But only an inch higher than what I'd already cleared. Half the length of my pinky finger. Surely I could do it.

I rocked from my heels to the balls of my feet, back and forth, concentrating on breathing, on stilling my mind. Then I took off, my arms pumping, feeling adrenaline rush through me, and burst upward with all the power in my left leg. I could feel it—a height I'd never been before. In the split second as my body reached the highest peak and began arching out across the bar, I heard these words, whispered quietly in my ear: *You could clear six feet easy.*

    L o r i   L .   L a k e

Then I piked and kicked and landed. The bar shivered and bounced. Click. It bounced again. Click. In slow motion, it slipped off the posts and fell toward me.

Ahhhhhh . . .

The spectators let out the same sound I heard in the rushing of my ears.

I don't know how I knew right then and there that I'd just jumped my best, but sure enough, I missed my second and third attempts. And so did Eliza. We both jumped out, setting a state record of five feet nine inches.

When the time came for presentation of the awards, she bent down to have the golden first place medal placed around her neck, and I got the silver. Second Place State Champion.

That was my last meet with Mark Collins as my coach. He took me aside on the last day of school and told me he had accepted a job in another state, at a school nearer his wife's family.

"I'm real sorry, Chris. I've been so proud to coach you. I *know* you can top six feet or more." He took some sheets of paper out of his back pocket and unfolded them. "Believe in yourself, and we'll hope a good coach gets hired. In the meantime, take these." He handed the sheets to me. "I've written out everything for your summer program and for next season, starting with week one and increasing your workouts until you're ready for the next State Meet. And there's my new address and phone." He pointed to the bottom of the last page. "Call me or write anytime you want."

I tried to follow Coach Collins' instructions, but my heart wasn't in it. Even though I qualified again for the State Meet the following year, I sprained my back two weeks before the competition and didn't attend. The only consolation was that no one broke the record. Seven years passed before anybody tied it.

Near the end of our senior year, Katie turned eighteen and eloped with her boyfriend. Last I heard, she was raising twins in a comfortable split-level tract house in the Cincinnati suburbs, while her husband managed a dog-racing track.

I dreamed of Katie for years as I walled myself off from other women and kept my feelings to myself. That is, until I met Margaret at a fundraiser against domestic violence. We began to meet for coffee every week or so, and then we started going to dinner together every Friday night. From the moment we first met, she seemed to see inside me and understand my fears. She sensed things about me I thought I'd hidden so completely no one would ever know. But she wasn't pushy and didn't probe deeply, allowing me to talk about things as I was ready.

One night at her house, sitting on the couch after an evening of manicotti and conversation, she reached out to me, and I leaned into her arms. She held me tight as a little voice inside my head whispered, "You're in over your head." I shooed the thought away and hugged her back.

That night, lying safe in the four-poster bed next to Margaret, I dreamt of Coach Collins.

At first, I was alone jogging around the track at my old high school. The gym door opened, and Coach Collins motioned toward me. His gesture said, "Come here."

I cut across the blacktopped running lanes, through the grass and over to the gym. I followed him through the door and up to the very top of the wooden bleachers. The building was silent and smelled of mold and old sweat socks. We sat next to one another on the top bench. He didn't have to say a word; I already knew he was leaving. For a moment, I wanted to cry, but I couldn't stand the idea of him seeing me weep.

He patted me and said, "Chris, you're still afraid of the bar."

My eyes filled with tears as I nodded.

"Everybody is afraid of the bar," he said. "It's okay, Chris. Everyone's *always* been afraid and always will be—it's normal." He smiled and reached out to pat my shoulder. "Believe me, you're fine."

I sat there on the hard bleacher in shock. I wanted to ask him how he knew this, how he could know I was fine, but I couldn't speak. He took my hands in both of his as he stood. I could feel the warmth of his fingers, and then he let go and stepped back. I caught my breath, thinking he would fall down the bleachers, but instead, he floated upward, one hand raised in a farewell greeting, and dissolved into nothingness.

After junior year when Eliza Schmidt and I set the state record, I never jumped over my head again—except in my dreams. Sometimes in the night, I still dream I'm alone, facing a high jump pit with a bar placed a foot over my head. Sometimes I am barefoot and can't jump. Or I do jump, but I land squarely on the bar and break my ribs or back.

Sometimes in those dreams, I fly through the air and the pit drops away, leaving me to fall screaming into an endless pit, until I wake up with a start and reach out to touch Margaret to steady myself.

But every once in a while, I make the approach, plant my left foot, and burst into the air, feeling power in my hair and a charge up my spine. I arch and pike, and from three feet above, I look down to see the black-and-white bar unmoving, resting untouched on the posts. And then I fall past it into the dark blue pit, as wide and enveloping as the ocean, and at that moment, I am not afraid.

About the Author

Lori L. Lake is the author of a dozen novels and two short story collections. She's edited four anthologies, including *Lesbians on the Loose* with Jessie Chandler, which won a Golden Crown Literary "Goldie" Award. Her short work is featured in over a dozen anthologies including *The Silence of the Loons, Time's Rainbow,* and *Women of the Mean Streets.*

Lori is known for sharing writing craft resources and is especially fond of teaching about crime fiction, short stories, and the craft of novel writing. In her spare time, she runs a small publishing house called Launch Point Press. Lori lives right at the edge of Portland, Oregon, in the Fortress of Solitude/Sanctuary of Solace. http://www.LoriLLake.com